FRAT SEX 2

EDITED BY
SEAN FISHER

alyson books
NEW YORK

© 2008 by Alyson Books. All rights reserved

Manufactured in the United States of America

Published by Alyson Books
245 West 17th Street, New York, NY 10011

Distribution in the United Kingdom by
Turnaround Publisher Services Ltd.
Unit 3, Olympia Trading Estate, Coburg Road, Wood Green
London N22 6TZ England

First Edition: September 2008

08 09 10 11 12 13 14 15 16 17 a 10 9 8 7 6 5 4 3 2 1

ISBN-10: 1-59350-093-9
ISBN-13: 978-1-59350-093-1

Library of Congress Cataloging-in-Publication data are on file.

Cover design by Victor Mingovits

Contents

Introduction

Frat boys are one of the world's most fascinating creatures. They have the uncanny ability to rule over a college campus—always. No one hesitates to respond to their roar when they throw a kegger, and we are all too willing to throw ourselves at their mercy. You can always tell who they are without them announcing it because they have a certain presence: wide pecs and a know-it-all grin. They're cocky and will no doubt try to charm you with their looks and street smarts. You can try to resist, but they only like a good fight and only get you more worked up. When it comes to frat boys, no one ever questions their sexuality despite the fact they roughhouse shirtless and all live together in one house. If they do this in front of us, can you imagine what goes on behind closed doors? I can, and so can Alyson Books. That's why we are continuing the *Frat Sex* series with this anthology.

Every gay man out there wishes frat boys were gay on some level. Personally, I don't like to think of them as straight or gay. I like to see them as toys of satisfaction—wild beasts made to quench our deepest fantasies. If there is something that frat boys know how to do very well, it's to be sexy. It is an inherent trait of all of them. They were built for one purpose: to make us want them.

In this anthology, you'll read about the desires of fraternity boys and their late-night escapades. Whether it is in Zachary Chase's "A Frat Boy for the Generations," where a frat boy yearns for a former brother who became his professor, or in Rob Rosen's "Initiation Night," where you'll get to see what happens on the most important night of frat boys' lives, these stories are rich and telling. We hope you find someone to connect with, because these brothers are laying it all out on the table for you.

—Sean Fisher

Laundry Room Lust

Bearmuffin

The laundry room of the Delta Gamma Beta fraternity was located two floors down in the basement. Far away from prying eyes, it turned out to be the perfect place for fucking and sucking with my frat brothers. This I discovered one hot evening when I decided to do my laundry. I had stripped down to my jockstrap and already started the washer when I saw Mike Maslowski's dirty jockstrap lying on the floor. I could tell because his name was written in black marker on the waistband. I grabbed the stinking jock and mashed it against my face. Oh, fuck. Mike was the hottest stud on the varsity wrestling team. Yeah, he was one piping hot stack of ass, all right. He was nineteen, tall, and packed with hot, sizzling muscle. He had deep-ditch abs, powerhouse biceps, and mighty tree-trunk thighs.

It only took about thirty seconds of his sizzling man-scent to make me rock hard! The pouch was still damp from a full day's sweat. It was stretched out of shape from Mike's huge cock and heavy balls! His ball-scent was pure heaven! I snorted in a few long breaths through the damp webbed pouch. It took me all of ten minutes to suck out all of that sweet-ass jock's man-scent. I felt my cock rise and stiffen. I looked down to see my cock bob up and down. I had a raging boner! So I grabbed my whizzer and began to fist it.

I shut my eyes and thought about Mike—his firm, juicy bubble butt encircled by a jockstrap, his wrestling singlet glued to him like a second skin, and his hot, muscular body dripping with sweat, just like it always did after a wrestling match. Pretty soon my harsh grunts were bouncing off the walls. I was fantasizing so hard about Mike that I didn't notice him walking in. "Like sniffing my jock, huh?"

When I opened my eyes Mike was standing in front of me. A shock of golden brown hair swept across Mike's wide forehead, grazing lightly over his sparkling deep green eyes. A wild smile creased his rugged lantern-jawed face. His red wrestling singlet was stretched lewdly over his wonderfully muscled body. He was hot and sweaty, just as I had imagined. "Just finished practice. Can I wash my uniform?" Before I could answer, Mike stripped off his wrestling singlet. Now he was standing in his jockstrap, white tube socks, and wrestling shoes. His cock and balls made a huge, tempting bulge between his thighs. I wanted to rip off his jock, kneel down, and suck on his gorgeous cock.

"If you don't wash your jock, Mike," I said teasingly, "I'll tell Coach." "Fuck!" Mike laughed. He slipped off his jock and dropped it into the washer. Mike's cock soared into the air. It boing-oinged like an arrow hitting the bulls-eye. My greedy lips trembled when I saw pre-come drops seeping from his piss slit. "I'm fuckin' horny, dude," Mike said. And so was I!

I grabbed Mike and slam-dunked my tongue into his mouth. The jock-stud reciprocated with equal passion. Our tongues battled while I caressed his smooth, brawny chest. "Oh, baby . . . oh, baby . . ." Mike moaned and grunted with macho pleasure as my hands slowly and ever so deftly glided down over his spectacular washboard abs and then back up again to land on his rock-hard chest. I took one juicy eraser-thick nipple between my fingers and fine-tuned it. "Awww, yeah," Mike whimpered, his voice blatantly thick with lust. The blond jock-god responded by slamming his raunchy crotch on my sweaty groin. "I wanna fuck . . . I wanna fuck," he kept saying to me. Mike fiercely humped his cock against mine.

Mike stuck his warm tongue inside my ear. I moaned and squirmed with pleasure. My hands automatically flew to his hard, humpy butt and I began caressing his lean, golden globes. When I slid one of my fingers into his asscrack, Mike moaned deeply in my ear, "I love it when you play with my ass!" Then he bent his head down and bit into my neck, his teeth gently pulling at the sensitive flesh under my ear. Lightly, he flicked my nipples with the tip of his rough tongue while he caressed my cock.

"I love your big fat cock," he whispered hotly. I began shaking with lust. He stroked the shaft once more and returned to the head, cupping it with his fingers. He sighed deeply while he made corkscrew motions against the tip. I threw my head back and gasped. I could feel the pre-come seeping from my hole. When Mike began sucking on nipples, I thought I was about to shoot my wad. Hot raw lust surged through me. My head was spinning. Here I was in the laundry room making it with the hottest dude on the wrestling team. I plunged my tongue into Mike's hot mouth again. Then I grabbed his thick uncut ten inches and fisted it with a savage, lust-mad fury I'd never felt before.

"Awww, fuck, dude," Mike growled. I jacked off the horny wrestler until his cock was solid and hot like a fiery poker. His eyes were clenched, his chest heaving, his breath escaping from his sensuous lips in long, deep blasts. Mike opened his eyes and looked at me with a pleading urgency. "Dude . . . suck me off . . . suck my fucking cock!" So I bowed over Mike's furry groin and went down on him. I took his cock right to the root. The minute Mike felt my lips wrap around his meat, he howled.

"Yeah!!! Suck my cock, stud . . . suck that fucker!" He humped forward and began pumping hard into my mouth. "Aw, fuck! Eat it, dude . . . eat my fuckin' cock!" Mike fastened his powerful hands around my head as he shoved his huge come-stinking-hung cock completely down my gasping throat. Hot tears welled in my eyes as I gagged and choked on his hot, pumping meat. I could barely breathe. Hot sweat began to stream from my fore-head into my eyes. Mike was screaming and moaning in complete, utter ecstasy. I wanted the stud to blast his hot fuckin' load down my throat. But actually Mike wanted to buttfuck me.

"C'mon, dude," he said, wrenching his cock from between my greedy lips. "Lend me your ass!" I quickly turned around and grabbed the dryer for support. I reached around and pulled my cheeks apart. "Fuckin A!" Mike howled as he stuck a finger up my asshole. My hole was pretty tight. And my ass muscles instantly sucked hard around his probing finger. "Dude! You got a tight butt! I'm gonna stick my cock up your ass!" I pushed my ass back and spread my cheeks as wide as I could get them. A cool blast of air rushed against my hole. I knew it was wide enough to drive a semi through it.

"Wow!" Mike gasped. He kneeled down and stuck his face in my hole. I was happily surprised to discover that Mike loved to eat ass. He grunted like a pig, mashing his blunt nose into my hole, running his tongue all over my crack. Mike really chowed down on my butt, licking and rimming it real good. His big, thick tongue felt like heaven on my crack. I fisted my cock while he rimmed me. Then he forced me down and mounted me. "I'm gonna ride ya, dude! I'm gonna really plow your fuckin' hole!

Mike shoved his cock all the way up my hole. I screamed. With a hefty grunt, Mike grabbed my shoulders for support. I was in agony but I pushed back so that his cock could slide all the way down my hole. Soon the searing streams of pain became waves of unadulterated macho pleasure. I soon relaxed and let Mike ride my ass like a bucking bronco. "Unngh . . . unngh . . . unngh . . . yeah, that's it . . . that's the way," he grunted. "Fuck my cock, dude. Keep on moving your ass like that. I like it!"

I used my expert ass-muscles to milk Mike's cock. He slammed his bull-wanger to the root. I threw my head back and screamed, bucking wildly, almost tossing him off. But Mike was too firmly impaled inside of me and he held on for dear life. "Yaaa-hooooooooo! Hot ass, dude, ya got a hot fuckin' ass!" I clamped my anus-ring around the root of his cock. Mike gasped with pleasure. "You're making me come, dude. I'm gonna come . . . I'm gonna fuckin' shoot up your ass!" A few more squeezes and Mike was ready to blast off. "Unnngh . . . unnngh . . . unngh . . . YO! YO!!! YO!!!! . . . awwwwwwwwww muuuuuutherrrrrfuuuuuuu-uckkkkkkkkkkk!"

Mike yanked out his cock from my hole and squirted his hot load all over my sweaty back. The come felt like hot lava scorching my skin. I gasped and howled as the come continued to pump out, drenching my back with his hot spurting jizz, dribbling down my neck and over my sides. Suddenly I leaped up and jumped Mike and pinned him, just like we were going to wrestle. "Whooooooooaa, dude!" Mike hit the floor and I went right down on his cock, drawing it between my lips as I pinched his nipples hard. Mike was a horny motherfucker. He had plenty of spunk. I knew he'd be ready to blast another hot load.

I dug into his sensitive nipples, pulling the flesh out and letting them snap against his barrel chest. Mike was thrashing and screaming. "Do it harder . . . harder!!!! . . . pinch hard . . . . ah, fuck . . . . I fuckin' love it!" I'd been fantasizing about Mike's humpy ass for long time. And now I was going to get a good taste of his hole. So I lifted Mike's mighty legs over his head and attacked his ass. I shoved my tongue all of the way up his stinking shit-chute. Mike

howled, "Yoooooooooooo! Wooooooowwwwwwww! Yoooooo-
ooooo! DUDE!!!! That's fuckin' hot!" Mike squirmed. He grunted hard. I gave his beautiful asshole a complete rimming until I
left him gasping for breath. "You win . . . you win . . . fuck my ass,
dude! Fuck my hole!"

I wanted to eat his ass some more so I stuck my face all the way
up his ass. I felt as if my head would disappear into his hot stinking butt. Mike thrashed around, his spit-drooling mouth wide
open as his golden-maned head slammed back and forth. "Fuck
me with your big stud-pud," he screamed. "Fucking split me in
half!" "Fuckin' A!," I screamed as I viciously shoved all of my ten
inches up his humping, tight jock-stud butt. His hot ass was so
fucking tight I had to struggle to get my cock up his hole. My cockhead banged against his tight anus-ring.

"Noooooooooo, dude . . . nooooooooooo, please . . . you're
gonna rip me wide open!" Mike's face was a mask of pain. Tears
were streaming down his face. And again and again I battered
against his rubbery asshole. But still he didn't ask me to stop. I
leaned over and bit right into one of his nipples. "Yaaaaaaaa-
rrrrrrrrrrghhhhhhhhhhh . . . fuccccccckkkkkkkkkkkkk!" Mike bellowed, his hands digging into my back as his hot asshole suddenly snapped wide open so that the full length of my cock hurtled
up his shit-chute.

It felt so fuckin' good to be inside him. His hole was tight,
steamy, and slick. I felt his ass-muscles suck around my cock and
gently massage the shaft. I held my cock for a few minutes up his
hole. And then I started pumping him hard. "Yeah . . . yeah . . .
yeah," he whimpered, getting into the fuck. I plowed harder, lifting his butt and slamming my groin against his. Mike was
snarling, gashing his teeth, whipping his head from side to side.
"Dude! You're a champ . . . you're a fuckin' champ!"

Laundry Room Lust

I was fucking Mike so goddamn hard his head was banging on the floor. Our wild, passionate, lusty yells bounced off walls. "Fuck me raw, dude . . . fuck my fag ass! FUCK IT!!!!" It was so fuckin' hot watching that big blond beauty bounce around like a rag doll with my cock up his ass. He had his eyes shut, his teeth were clenched. I knew he was enjoying getting butt-fucked. I quickly rolled Mike head over heels. His thick bronzed feet flew up over his head. His fist clamped around his pre-come drooling cock. Mike began fisting it wildly in complete and total sync with my maniacal pounding thrusts. I had my cock to the fucking hilt up his stinking jock ass.

I rammed it in and out, from side to side. Our bodies were a wild blur. His moans soon became screams of pleasure. Hearing Mike moan like a big pussy made it all worthwhile. Mike opened his beautiful blue eyes and looked right at me. "Shoot your spunk, dude. Shoot it now. 'Cause I'm gonna come . . . gonna fuckin' come!" I felt my balls ready to erupt. "Ready for my load, fucker?" I screamed at him. "Yeah, dude!" "Ready for some hot spunk up your tight ass?" I yelled. "Yeah!" he panted. "Give it to me, dude . . . SHOOT YOUR LOAD!!!" "Unnngh . . . unnngh . . . unnngh . . . awwwwwwww fuuuuuuuuckkkkkinnnnnn' AA-AAAAAAAAAAA!"

With a hot shudder, we both came at the same time. I could feel my hot come shooting inside Mike's ass in a continuous stream. Mike's gorgeous, muscular body went into spasms, his hot fuck blasting from his cock, drenching our abs. I pulled out my cock and squirted all over him, dousing Mike's face and chest with my hot come. He looked up and smiled at me, my sizzling come dribbling down his handsome face. Then Mike fished his wrestling singlet and jockstrap out of the dryer and slipped them on. He said, "That was a hot fuck, dude! See ya!" and dashed upstairs.

Later I was back in my room and still horny. But I still had Mike's dirty jockstrap, so I give it a good whiff and began pounding my pud. Once again, I fantasized about him. Fuck! It was like Mike was standing there right in front of me. "If only," I sighed as I squirted another hot load all over myself.

A Frat Boy for the Generations

Zachary Chase

The first thing I noticed about Professor Bradshaw was how vulnerable his crotch looked in his jeans. Even when he'd clap chalk off his hands, I'd follow the white dust down to the bulge coming out of his pants. It was a tight bulge, and the air around it always lay still and undisturbed as though it were too proud to be anywhere else on his body. During lecture, I'd sometimes fantasize about sucker punching his crotch just to see how sensitive it was and watching as he'd fall cringing to the floor, red-faced, with his mouth wide opened, gasping in pain.

Professor Bradshaw was beautiful. I'm not just talking about his physical beauty because he was more than an object to me. He was exactly what a man should be and the bulge between his pants seemed to be the essence of all that. But he also had these eyes about him; they were very oval and glossy with a distinct shade of blue. It seemed as though his eyes had the ability to look right through me and see the truth. I felt I belonged to him, because he had figured me out. The way he looked at me when I raised my hand in class, he knew I had a crush on him.

He wasn't that much older than the traditional college student. In fact, he had been a fraternity brother of mine three years before, when I was a freshman. He was still part of the fraternity as our faculty sponsor and always came to our events. And by events, I mean keggers. He was still a California State College student enrolled in the Marketing Department's doctoral program, and was teaching a few introduction to marketing courses. So of course, I wasn't the only one who liked him. It was obvious all the girls in our class had a thing for him. At our fraternity parties, they would always go up to him half drunk. He wouldn't touch them, but their obnoxious giggling clearly said they wanted him. I got jealous when they stayed after class asking dumb questions about assignments that were self-explanatory. I bet they only wanted him because he came across so strong and invincible. I wasn't like them—I would conquer him and let him know what true pleasure felt like. Those girls just wanted his attention and it pissed me off, because from the moment I saw him, I knew a part of him would be mine.

But his appeal wasn't only to the girls. You could tell the straight guys dug him, too. For starters, he wasn't strict about attendance or giving boring AM lectures. He taught basic marketing concepts with these sports analogies. He was so simple and macho in his teaching, you couldn't help but see him as a frat guy who happened to be a teacher. Now, I'm not a sports fan. Ever since I came out of the closet, I stopped pretending to care about sports. Even when my fraternity went to football games, I always made up an excuse to stay behind at the house. But it was the way he used the analogies that got me horny. It was as if he didn't know any other way to teach, and it was just so damn cute. Even when dividing the class up into groups, there were boys and there were girls. He would say, "Okay, boys, this is the hardest lesson you'll have to learn: how to function without girls. Guys on one side of the room, girls on the other." It just made him more adorable that he didn't acknowledge anything beyond heterosexuality or sports. Perhaps adorable isn't the right word, but it made him comes across as sheltered and vulnerable to the big bad world. I like to think I could see right through him, too. Right through his tough-guy facade and see the point of his vulnerability—his bulge. God, I remember just wanting to see him in only his underwear, lying right in front of me with his thighs spread wide open while the palm of my hand massaged his crotch.

I was the only guy who sat in the front row of the class. I wanted to be as close as possible to him just to admire his body. You could tell he worked out really hard to maintain his shape because his chest came right out of the tight polo shirts he wore. He had the classic looks of a 1950s beefcake model, which is to say he had a baby face with massive pecs, bulky arms, and shaped calves. What gave me hope that he wasn't totally straight was his hair: it was perfectly spiked. There was no way he could have just styled it out of the shower.

For the first few weeks of class, I like to think we shared a special connection. He knew I was a fellow Sigma Chi brother, and I'm also pretty sure he knew I was gay. I was the only openly gay frat brother to date in my chapter, so I was big news. For the most part, my frat brothers were okay with it. I think if Professor Bradshaw were in my fraternity now, he would probably not give it a second thought, but there was something that was repressed about him. He was sophisticated and had a street-smarts wit to him, but his posture gave away he had come from a conservative background. He always stood with his chest flexed, and his fists always clutched together. When he was lost in thought, he'd always punch his palm with his fist.

Before class started, he'd smile at me and ask, "Kyle, where did we leave off last session?" Despite having a whole row of girls with their textbooks already open, he singled me out. Now maybe that meant nothing, but it wasn't just that. Some of the answers on my test that we were clearly wrong were marked right. Later on, he told me it wasn't a coincidence.

So I'll just come out and say it: we hooked up. Cliché, right?

But that's not the point of my story; it's what he did to me . . . or rather, what I did to him that matters. The day we hooked up, there was a thunderstorm. I was running to class, splashing mud all over the sidewalk, when I noticed how green leaves look when they're drenched. I had gotten to class unusually early, but the session before me must have cancelled class because the room was empty except for whatever light could escape the gray sky. I put my head down at my desk and closed my eyes, concentrating only on the sound of the air conditioning. I started to drift into fantasy and was thinking of Professor Bradshaw running to his office, himself drenched in water. He'd be taking off his shirt and wrapping his arms around his hard nipples just to stay warm. I started to think of him caressing his nipples and flicking them with the tip of his index finger. I was getting hard and the head of my cock was already wet with pre-come. I don't know how long I was fantasizing, but I came out of it once I started to hear a buzzing sound. I opened my eyes and saw a fly frantically trying to lift itself off my desk, but it kept crashing back down. After a few tries, it zigzagged through the air for a few seconds, until it finally gave up and fell back down to die. As I stared at it, I thought about never being able to touch Professor Bradshaw or even get to know him. It was a strong feeling of dread and I began to get uncomfortable in my seat.

The door flung open and I heard the washed out voices of people in the hall coming through. I lifted my head, and Professor Bradshaw entered. He wasn't drenched but wearing a yellow raincoat and jeans with an umbrella in his hands.

"Ah, damn it," he said. "Don't tell me no one's going to show just 'cause of the rain."

I really didn't know what to say. I had never been alone in a room with him.

"I don't think rain is a big attendance motivator," I said.

Professor Bradshaw chuckled. It was a light chuckle, but still something. I looked at my watch and it was already time for class to begin.

"I tell you what," he said. "Why don't we just cancel class and you can get a head start going back to the house. I know you guys have to plan for homecoming next month and that is going to be a huge event for us."

"Not going to argue," I said, quickly grabbing my bag. It was weird—for all the fantasies I had about him, I didn't want to stay alone in the room with him. I was afraid of not seizing the moment with him or failing to bond over something. All my frat brothers always seemed to bond with him except me and I just wanted to run out of the classroom so I wouldn't feel like I couldn't. I was just too awkward around him and it was easier to leave. As I started to walk out the door, something in me kicked. It was a brief second, but I knew what I wanted. I stopped before I opened the door.

"Hey, Professor," I said. "I have a question on the assignment due next week."

"What about it?" he responded. Thunder crashed outside but the room was dead silent. I didn't know what I asking but I knew what I was becoming.

"Something ab-ab-about," I began to stutter. "About . . . I just don't get the difference between product modification and product redefining."

"What didn't you get?" he asked.

"The stuff after the word product." I said with my eyes wide open.

I expected Professor Bradshaw to laugh or make eye contact with me. I was trying to be cute, but he didn't respond. Instead he pulled a paper out of his bag. "Kyle, if you give me five minutes to write a sign for the door and make sure no one else shows up, we'll go up to my office and talk about it. I just don't want to stay here longer than I have to."

Something in his voice was different. It sounded overly serious as if he knew something was coming.

"Cool," I said. "I'll just wait over here or something."

We walked up to his office in silence; the only noise we heard was the repeated thunder crashes from outside. His office was small, no windows, and void of any decorations; just a plain desk with a table lamp and a computer. The walls were warm looking and it was nice to be shielded from having to look at the storm outside.

"Okay, product modification and redefining," he said clicking the mouse on his computer.

"Oh, there you go with that crazy marketing jargon again," I said nervously.

Again he didn't react. He just sat there, looking at his computer with his blue eyes. I felt he didn't even want me in there. I was afraid that he already knew the real reason why I had asked him for help and was annoyed by it. He began to type feverishly. I was amazed at how fast and powerful his fingers looked on the keyboard.

"I think you need to see some real-world examples," he said. "Pull the chair from the corner and we'll give you some examples."

He looked right at me for a second and then motioned to the chair. I felt ridiculous; I could feel that tingly feeling of shame between my legs.

A Frat Boy for the Generations

"All right, let's look at Nike shoes and their ads as an example," he said as I sat next to him.

I knew the difference between product modification and redefining; in fact, the definitions were in the glossary of our textbook. He also must have known I wasn't serious because I'd gotten an A on everything in his class.

"So, okay," I said. "Product modification is when you make changes to a product in the market?"

Professor Bradshaw smiled at me, "Almost. It's when they want to expand the lifespan of the product." He smelled fresh, like he had just come out of the shower. He began to go into details about a product lifecycle and then—out of nowhere—I felt his foot getting closer to mine. My heart did a double beat. I wasn't sure what was going on, but he kept explaining the definitions to me. I could hear my heart pounding in my ears now and my crotch growing bigger. I felt the motion of his sneaker right in front of my muddy shoes. Was he doing this on purpose or was I just looking for a glimmer of hope? My thoughts were racing a thousand miles per hour and I could not grasp them. I couldn't think; all I could do was react. I reacted quite intimately by moving my foot closer to his until our shoes were kissing, the dried mud at the tip of my shoe rubbing up against his. I was being coy. Maybe some of my other frat brothers would have been more aggressive in a situation like this, but I didn't know how to be that anywhere else but in my fantasies.

He put his arm on my chair and turned around to me. His leg was shaking and we looked at each other for a few seconds. My dick had grown fully hard by now and I was pretty sure I was about to come all over myself. I couldn't believe this was happening. He stepped on my foot and leaned in closer to me, starting to breathe rapidly on my face. I did the next step, and went right in and kissed him. He tasted sweet, like I was wrapping strawberry flavor around my mouth. His tongue began sweeping mine and I began to realize I never would have expected that from Professor Bradshaw in my fantasies. It seems that these little details in his movement were things I never thought about. He then got up from his chair.

"Don't tell anyone," he said.

He started squeezing my shoulder as if it were a piece of clay for him to mold. I thought he would have been a bit more intimate with me or more dependent on my touch. He slammed my body on the floor and stood over me. It was as though he were treating me like one of his buddies and roughhousing with me. Maybe this is what he did with the other frat brothers? I tried to get up, but he smirked at me, as if I were insignificant and pushed my chest down with little effort. I wanted him to forfeit his body over to me, but he wouldn't. He was the one in control and I had no strength to topple him.

He hovered over me, examining my body. The bulge in his pants was distinct and I reached out for it, but he grabbed my wrist and threw my arm back. I felt like the vulnerable one now. I was sacrificing something inside of me to him—something he wouldn't care to have. He motioned for me to unbutton my shirt, and I did.

"Nice abs," he told me, pulling a condom out his wallet. "Really nice."

He reached into his back pocket and pulled out his wallet. It was a black wallet, so simple looking no one would ever give it a second look. He then showed me a condom.

"Wait one second," he said. "I don't want anyone to hear us."

He moved over to his computer and clicked around until the

computer started playing a song I had never heard before. He lifted his chin up and with a big smirk said, "I love this song."

The song's guitar made the yellow paint on the walls become warmer and the air around us started to smell more like a classroom on the first day of class. He started licking my stomach, his tongue sucking the flavor off my skin. I started to thrust my hips and my cock was rubbing up against his bulge. His penis was still tucked away in the zipper, but the head of my cock was popping out of my jeans.

He started to take off my pants, but was showing no signs of taking any of his clothes off. "I have to get ready for a class soon," he told me. "Let's get to it." He didn't kiss me, he didn't even hug me. I was getting impatient. I wanted something from him, something that would leave him helpless, instead of the dominance he was robbing away from me that made him stronger.

"Wait," I said, turning around to him and trying to kiss his neck.

"No kissing," he said, slamming me back down. He started gripping my thighs, moving his way to my boxers. He wasn't speaking to me or saying anything. It occurred to me that I didn't even know what kind of person Professor Bradshaw was; all I had were my fantasies. He started to remove my boxers and my cock was literally vibrating with sensation from the excitement. Then he carefully took off his polo, much to my surprise. He was trying to make sure not to ruin his hair as he lifted it over his head, and then I finally saw his body. It was beefy, just like I had predicted. He had muscles; I'm talking chiseled pecs and a V-cut pelvis. I don't know why he was so impressed with my abs because his were clearly more defined. I started to jerk off. I wanted to come and I began rubbing it up.

"Not so fast," he said, flipping me over and spreading my ass.

He stayed quiet for a few seconds, it sounded like he was putting the condom on, but I couldn't see it. He lifted my legs up and before I knew it, I was in a wheelbarrow position and the blood was rushing to my head. I didn't have the strength to hold myself, but I kept going because I wanted to know the real Professor Bradshaw. I turned my ear to the side and heard him mumbling lyrics. Then, I felt him ramming his dick in me like a car crashing into a wall. It was raw, but I think he had used some lube when I turned around. He wasn't being gentle and he didn't even give me a chance to look at his cock before he shoved it in. I could feel it, though—he couldn't deny me that. It was thick and very long. I turned to look at him and his eyes were closed; his breathing coming in through his mouth. Finally, though, I felt he was giving me something and that we were connected somehow. Now, we had a piece of history together that could not be erased. He let my legs go and clutched his hands ahold of my butt, squeezing it. I couldn't keep my posture too long and I started to tumble.

"Come here," he said, pulling me back as he sat himself down on his chair. He wrapped his arm around my stomach and lifted me up onto his lap. I dug my fingers onto his knees and noticed he still had his jeans on. The song had ended by this time and there was nothing but the sound of our breaths and the squeaky chair. I was starting to moan as he kept thrusting it deeper and deeper in me. I couldn't stop moaning, I knew someone one could probably hear me but I just didn't care. I had envisioned his body being more passive than mine. Instead, his body was aggressive— making sure I was properly secured and comfortable and, to be honest, it was feeling good to be taken over. I was never a fan of being a bottom, but he was hitting all the right spots. I really couldn't stop moaning and Professor Bradshaw cupped his hand over my mouth to stop me from making any more noises.

A Frat Boy for the Generations

My body was in a state of ecstasy and I wanted to cry into his hands and tell him how much I needed him. I started to see a flash of images in my heads. I was remembering how strong his fingers looked on the keyboard and how he would punch his palm during class. I started to suck on his fingers, breathing my dominance onto his hand. I could feel his fingers wiggling in my mouth, trying to get free. I didn't want to let them go, and bit them so they would stop moving. He then gave me a slight slap on the cheek with his other hand.

"Be good," he said, forcing his hand out of my mouth and onto my shoulder for leverage. He started thrusting and the chair began to wheeze hysterically.

"I'm going to do it," he said. I turned around to look at him. His eyes were still closed and his face was pointed up, his hair looking like a mountain waiting to be climbed.

"Yeah, keep going. Keep going," I said

"I'm coming," he said.

When he came, the sound of the thrusting started to sound smoother as if our motions were in sync, and eventually the squeaking from the chair slowly died out. Once he was done, he pulled me closer to him and dug his face into my back as he wrapped his arms around me. He gave me a discreet kiss on my neck, as if he accidentally did it. He lifted me off his lap and set me down on the floor. I lay down, still hard and confused.

"Are you going to finish up?" he asked, taking the condom off his dick. I finally got to see it. It was powerful looking, probably one of the biggest I had ever seen. I could never have been prepared to take that if I had seen it before it went in.

"Can I get some help?" I asked.

"I'm not gay," he said, pulling his jeans up and sitting back onto his chair.

I didn't know what to say. I wasn't angry, but I was ashamed. I stretched my hand across the floor until I felt the metal steel of the chair I had been using. It had somehow ended up against the wall. The steel was cold, and I wrapped my hand around it for comfort.

"Just come close to me," I said. "Do me the favor."

He came down to me. "All right. What do you want me to do?" he asked, a southern accent escaping into his words. I had never noticed it so distinct before.

"Well, can you take your jeans off?" I asked. He looked at me, hesitant. I knew what his response was going to be.

"No," he replied, any trace of accent gone out of his voice again.

I sat up and tried to run my fingers through his hair, wanting him not to be afraid. I knew he was mine for a second, when his accent was loose. He had surrendered to me for that one second, and I wanted it back. I wanted to show him I could be the man and take care of him, but he grabbed my hand before I could run it through his hair.

"Can you just take your jeans off," I pleaded. "Let me see all of your body. I want mine to be like yours."

He stood up and took his shoes off. His pants were still unzipped, so he just rolled them down and stood in front of me in white briefs and tight black socks. I began jerking off. I didn't need much time because I was ready to come when he walked into the classroom. He must have gotten curious, because he placed his foot on my testicles, causing my body to get goose bumps. The texture of his sock made the sensation feel better, and my skin felt defenseless. I grabbed his foot and squeezed it as I came all over myself.

We kept hooking up for the next few weeks; sometimes it was after class in his office, but most of the time it was in the fraternity house. I noticed he couldn't get enough sex with me at the fraternity house and was always more liberal with his body in there, meaning he would let me stroke his dick or even suck it a few times. When I'd come home from class, he'd be with some of my brothers watching a game on the TV or playing ping-pong. I'd just go upstairs into my room. I hated seeing him with other men and I especially didn't want to think he was messing around with someone else. When I'd go to bed, that's when he'd sneak into my room and crawl into my bed. So he would be the one pursuing me—it wasn't like I was his stalker. There was one night in particular, a few weeks before the incident at homecoming, when he spent the entire night with me instead of leaving and going back to his apartment after he finished fucking me. Our entire fraternity had just gotten back from the beach. Sand was all over my bed and scratching my raw skin as we began laughing about a ridiculous know-it-all redheaded girl in our class. It got to a point where we both were laughing hysterically and very loud. I dug my head into his chest to muffle my laughter and that's when he put his arm around me and pulled my entire body closer to him. He didn't loosen his grip on me and I fell asleep on his tanned pecs. After that night, he was a bit more considerate to me in front of my frat brothers. I wasn't scrawny, but I wasn't as muscular as he, or, for that matter, most of my brothers. When we were assembling the homecoming day float for the parade, he would help me lift pieces of metal or hold my ladder as I was nailing. It was stupid stuff and no one really noticed except for me. However, he always treated me as submissive and I hated that at times. If I ever tried to roughhouse with him in front of the other boys, he'd just throw a weak punch at my arm and laugh me off.

Otherwise, things were going well. We weren't a couple, but we had a beat and would just always find a way to come together. I don't mean to sound cocky, but I knew he was starting to feel something for me. However, I was afraid it paled when compared to how he bonded with the other fraternity brothers. When homecoming day came, that's when everything changed—and not for the better.

I was getting ready for the parade. I was supposed to meet my brothers at the stadium where the parade would begin and go through the campus. I hadn't seen Professor Bradshaw for a week since the university had an irregular schedule during homecoming week. I was putting on my college jersey when he came into my room holding a plastic bag in his hand, which he quickly tossed onto my bed.

"Hey," he said.

He looked upset, really nervous and agitated. His eyes weren't as oval; instead they squinted in shame. I haven't dated many guys before, but I know when they come in with a certain look. Especially the look Professor Bradshaw had, that made it seem as though he'd already grown tired of me.

"What's up?" I asked.

"Nothing," he said.

We stayed quiet for a few seconds, listening to the clunky air conditioner unit by my bed.

"Let's talk after the event," he said abruptly.

Professor Bradshaw was wearing a California State T-shirt with khaki shorts and flip-flops. He was like the perpetual frat boy. Why was I crushing on him so much?

"Whatever," I told him.

As we walked out of the house, I realized I was angry at him. I could never envision myself angry at Professor Bradshaw, and yet, I was fuming.

A Frat Boy for the Generations

The yellow and blue streamers flew through the sky as we began moving in our homecoming float throughout campus. I saw Professor Bradshaw with the other frat brothers. He was jumping on them while throwing silly string into the crowd. He didn't look like a professor but, rather, one of us. His smile was beautiful—I could tell he was having fun. But he hadn't spoken to me since we left the house. Wasn't he upset at all that we might be breaking up? I backed to a corner and started waving to the crowd, seeing girls being lifted up by their boyfriends and the guys all roughhousing with each other. Where did I fit in all of it? Here I was, in a lonely corner of my own fraternity's homecoming float. And then I saw her: the redheaded know-it-all from our class. She wasn't participating in the parade or with the crowd. Her face was grim and she was just reading a book as the people around her were jumping and drinking beer. No one was looking at her and she wasn't engaging with anyone. I realized at that moment that I didn't want to be like that. I didn't want to *be* her.

I turned my head to the float's main stage and saw my fraternity on top of it, roughhousing and yelling out to the crowd. I was witnessing the building blocks of male bonding, and I could never break into it, at least not in the way that would make Professor Bradshaw happy. I just didn't know how to be a frat boy or bond with any one of them. Then I saw something that horrified me. I couldn't explain it, but it triggered something in my head. One of my frat brothers jumped onto Professor Bradshaw's back, pushing him down to his knees on the floor. He grabbed Professor Bradshaw and started to give him a nuggie. He was dominating him. I know it wasn't in a sexual way, they were just rough, but Professor Bradshaw had become subordinate to him—something he never let me do to him. When Professor Bradshaw got up, he was red-faced, and quickly started feeling his hair to make sure all his spikes were still standing.

I didn't feel like celebrating once the parade was over. I was beyond jealous—I was fuming. I could almost feel smoke coming out of my ears. Even when frat row had become one big party I was still upset and refused to participate. I ran into our house and went upstairs to my room to cry. Everyone was outside on the streets, officially drunk at three o'clock in the afternoon. The music was loud and intensified my tears. I was burying my head into my pillow when I heard someone opening my door. I could hear the voice tucked away in the pounding bass from outside and knew it was him.

"Kyle," he said. "What's wrong?"

"Go away," I yelled.

"Look, I want to talk . . ." he replied.

The feeling of being inadequate began to take over my body; I knew what he was going to do. I wasn't man enough for him; he wanted a real frat boy. He was already going to move on, to someone stronger. To someone who would dominate him. I got up, in tears, and slapped him. I didn't give a warning or anything. Just bang, right across his beautiful face. I had no idea where that came from, but it fueled something in me. I began walking back to my bed but then turned back around to charge him. I punched him right in the nose, and he began to bleed from his nose as he stepped back in disbelief. I took that as my opening and began slapping his chest as rapidly as I could. However, he snapped out of his daze and was prepared for me. He just grabbed my body with one tight grip and started shaking me.

"What the fuck is wrong with you, Kyle?" he yelled at me. "Calm down! Let's talk about this!"

I knew what he wanted to talk about. It was obvious from the second he walked in, and from how he'd avoided me during the parade. I wasn't going to let him treat me as his bitch anymore. That's when I tested how sensitive his bulge was and kneed him right in the groin. His face turned red, just like in my fantasies. I don't know how hard I hit him, but he fell to the floor gasping in pain.

He lay there yelling "Fuck" over and over again, but no one could hear him. No reasonably straight frat brother was in the house and the music was making the walls vibrate. I knelt down before him and ran my fingers through his hair, messing it up; then I was gripping it so hard strands were coming out in my fingers. I pulled his face to me. He was red and his eyes were still watery from the pain. Then I whipped out my cock and started smacking his face with it. He grimaced and I began to stroke myself. It didn't take long for me to shoot all over his face. While I was coming he pushed me off him and gathered himself up to leave. I grabbed his foot before he could take off, trying to keep him down, but he maneuvered his foot out of his flip-flop and ran. I felt like the prince in Cinderella and started running after him with his shoe in my hand. I pulled my pants up and ran out the door, but I couldn't find him in the labyrinth of music and drunk college peers. And then I saw him running back to the campus, not looking back.

I went back upstairs to my room, in disbelief over what I had just done. I threw his flip-flop to the corner of my room and sat on my bed. Next to me was the plastic bag he had brought me. I opened it and found a box of Nike shoes in it. In fact they were the ones we had seen on his computer when I asked him the question about product modification after class. There was a yellow envelope. As I opened it and began to read I remembered the fly buzzing in the classroom the day we'd first hooked up.

"Kyle," the card read. I saw the fly in my head, buzzing. "I hope you understand the difference between product modification and product redefining." I saw the fly zigzagging, desperately fighting for life. "Because you've rebranded me completely." I saw the fly finally crashing and dying.

I held the card in my head, remembering that feeling of dread and knowing I finally had a piece of him, but would never have all of him again.

Friends and Lovers

Thom Jaymes

Tate forced his way through the crowd, careful not to spill his beer. He finally made it to the front door, grateful for the gush of fresh air that greeted him. Taking a deep breath, he settled in a plastic chair, relaxing for the first time since he had arrived at the party.

The sweat that had collected in his buzzed black hair grew cool in the evening air, sending a slight chill through his body. He ran a hand over his head, flicking the majority of it away.

"Get tired of dancing?" a familiar voice asked. He knew immediately that it was his best friend, Jennifer—the one responsible for him being at the party in the first place.

Tate smiled. "Never."

Jennifer hauled another chair over and sat down, propping her long legs up on Tate's lap. Her little blue dress was so short that Tate could easily see her underwear peeking out.

At least she's wearing some tonight, he thought. "Why are you out here?"

Jennifer grabbed the beer bottle out of Tate's hand. "I was getting bored." She took a sip, frowning as she swallowed. "God, that shit is nasty. I don't know how you can drink it."

Tate made a face, taking back the beer. "I think it's delicious. Well, the first couple aren't that great, but once you get around to the third or fourth, they taste pretty damn good."

Jennifer laughed. She shook her head, her long blond curls bouncing about. "You're a trip."

"So where's Jeff?"

Jeff was Jennifer's brother. Her twin, actually. Identical. He belonged to the fraternity hosting the party. He—in Tate's eyes anyway—was the perfect guy. Strong, handsome, kind, funny, intelligent, and with just the right amount of weirdness to make him interesting. He was always joking around with Tate about being gay. Not making fun of him—just pretending to flirt.

He was pretty much everything you could want in a guy. There was only one small thing wrong with him:

He was straight.

"He's playing some video game, I think. You know him. If there's a virtual monster of some sort that needs to be killed, he's there."

"Saving the day, one virtual beast at a time."

"Exactly."

"Has he decided if he's going to be moving into the frat house or not?" Tate asked.

"I don't know." Jennifer bit her lip, thinking. "I would think that he's going to stay at the house with us. I mean, considering dues and all, it would be cheaper for him."

"Yeah, but this is Jeff we're talking about. He's pretty impulsive."

Jennifer stood and adjusted her dress. "Oh, it's his decision, I guess. We can always find another roommate."

"Yeah." Tate took another swig from his beer. "There's a guy in one of my classes who's been wanting to move closer to campus. I could ask him."

"Sounds good to me." Jennifer bent down and kissed Tate on the cheek. "I think I'm going to head back to the house. It's getting late and I have class tomorrow morning. How about you?"

"No, I think I'll hang out a little bit longer."

"Suit yourself." With that, she stepped off the porch and started down the street.

Tate watched his friend disappear into the night. He drained his beer and stood, stretching his arms wide. In search of a trashcan, he ventured back into the party. Sure enough, the one located in the kitchen was overflowing onto the floor.

After deciding that the sink was as good a place as any to leave his bottle, Tate left the kitchen and started looking for Jeff.

After walking into two different rooms and finding couples groping one another, he found him upstairs, sprawled out on a bed, wildly thumbing away on a Nintendo controller.

Two other guys were in the room sitting in beanbag chairs. One guy Tate had never met before. The other was a stupid jock he had seen around campus several times. He could usually be observed arguing with his girlfriend. Apparently, from what Tate had overheard, at least, neither of them was able to be faithful to the other for more than two days at a time.

"Tate!" Jeff roared. "Where have you been?"

"Outside." Tate took a seat on the bed next to his friend. "Your sister went home."

"That's cool." Jeff sat up, bumping into Tate, then leaning against him. "You want to play?"

God, I'd love to play with you . . . "Eh, I'm not very good at video games."

"You don't have to be good to beat Jeff," the unfamiliar guy said. "He sucks."

"Fuck you, Aaron." Jeff grabbed a pillow and tossed it at the boy, hitting him in the chest. "Just because you own the damn game and get tons of extra practice, doesn't mean that I'm a shitty player."

"Whatever, man."

The theme song from *Family Guy* suddenly filled the room. The jock sat up, reached into his pocket and pulled out a cell phone. He held it out, showing Aaron who was calling.

"God, what does that whore want now, man?" Aaron asked.

"I don't care." He put the phone back into his pocket. "She just needs to understand that I'm not ready for a relationship right now."

"Your girlfriend?" Tate asked, curious.

"You could say that." The guy laughed and exchanged a high five with Aaron. "One of the many."

"That's cool, I guess." Tate bit his lip, not really knowing what to say.

The guy fell back into his beanbag. "You aren't getting it from more than one bitch, dude?"

"No."

"Oh, c'mon, are you *queer* or something?"

"Yes."

"Well, fuck then." The guy made a face. "Are you at least getting it from old Jeff here?"

Tate started to say something, but Jeff cut him off.

"Yeah. We fuck all the time. Like damn rabbits or some shit. It's wild. You should come over and watch it sometime."

Tate's face went red. He was used to Jeff joking about stuff, but never in front of anyone other than Jennifer or their close friends.

Aaron burst out laughing. "God, it all makes sense now. That's why you always want to come over and play games with us, Jeff. You're trying to get some fresh ass to tap."

"No, I'm satisfied with my man." Jeff threw his arms around Tate, dropping his controller on the floor. "He's all I need."

Jeff's breath washed over Tate's face. It smelled like he had brushed his teeth with rubbing alcohol. "God, how much did you have to drink?"

"He's had a lot," Aaron answered, pointing to an empty bottle of liquor on top of the TV. "We've been taking shots every time we lose a match. And, since he *sucks*, he's taken several."

"Piss off." Jeff grabbed his controller and turned his attention back to the game. "I'll beat this next guy."

Tate stared at the screen. It wasn't a game with which he was familiar, but it had something to do with boxing. He watched until one of the blocky men knocked the other down and started jumping up and down on his chest.

"Way to go, Jeff," the jock said. "You're getting your ass kicked again."

"Damn it. Screw this." Jeff tossed the controller to Aaron. "I'm going home." He stood up, stumbled, and fell back against the bed.

Both of Jeff's friends started laughing.

"Are you okay?" Tate asked.

Jeff glanced at his friend, a wild grin on his face. "I'm fine."

"Your *boyfriend* better walk home with you." Aaron said.

"He will." Jeff grabbed Tate's hand and tugged him off the bed.

Taking into account how drunk his friend was, Tate thought he might need to clear the air a little. Just in case one of these guys sobered up and decided they didn't want a fag—even a fake one—in their fraternity. "You guys know he's not my actual boyfriend, right?"

"Of course." Aaron tossed the controller aside. "He's just a big goof."

"Cool."

"Make sure he doesn't attract a lot of attention on your way home," the jock spoke up. "We don't need the cops coming around because they see old Jeff wandering around all fucked up."

Tate looked at his friend. His pale blue eyes were so watery it looked like he had been crying. "I'll do what I can." He laughed. "No promises, though."

They walked—or stumbled, in Jeff's case—home in silence. Tate was trying to think of something to talk about, but nothing came to mind. Fortunately, Jeff had something to say.

"Fuck, man. I've got to take a piss."

"We're almost home."

"I can't wait."

Jeff wandered away from the sidewalk and into the wooded area that lined both sides of the street leading back to their part of town.

Tate sighed and followed.

His friend stopped walking, leaned against a tree, and unzipped his pants.

Tate denied his first impulse to watch his drunken friend and looked away. The stillness of the night was interrupted only by the sound of Jeff's urine splattering on the ground. A short time later the splattering fizzled out.

"All done?"

"Yeah."

"Cool." Tate turned his attention back to Jeff and, even though he tried not to, his eyes instantly focused on his crotch. To his surprise, Jeff hadn't bothered to put his cock back in his jeans. "Dude, your shit's still out."

Jeff slumped against the tree, his thumbs going into his belt loops. A strange smile etched its way across his face, but he said nothing.

Tate fought the urge to reach out and take the dick in his hand. The desire to feel his friend's bare flesh make contact with his own was almost overpowering. "Come on, man. We need to get home."

"Suck my dick," Jeff said.

"What?"

"Suck my fucking dick, Tate."

"Jeff, I think—"

"Shut up." Jeff grabbed Tate by the arm and hauled him forward. "Get on your knees."

"No," Tate said, even though his legs were betraying him. He found himself on the ground, Jeff's cock inches from his face.

"Put your mouth on me."

"Jeff, what are you doing?"

"Tate, I don't want to talk. I want my dick sucked. You want to suck my dick. Let's just do it."

"I don't want to blow you, dude," Tate lied. *This is not happening. What the fuck is going on?*

"Bullshit."

"Jeff, even if I did want to, you're drunk."

"Tate!" Jeff shouted. "I fucking want you to do it. I want you to suck me. I want to know what it feels like."

"You're never gotten head before?" Tate asked. "You've dated like twelve different girls since I've known you." His own cock had swollen to full erection in his shorts, the pleasant pain of it pressing against his underwear forcing him to breathe slowly.

"That doesn't mean I've fucked around with all of them." Jeff shook his head hard from side to side, like he was trying to clear his mind. "I don't just want head, man. I want head from *you*."

"What?"

"I want to see what it's like from a guy."

"Dude—"

"Suck my cock."

"Jeff—"

"Suck it!"

Tate did as he was told, running his tongue along the length of Jeff's flaccid tool. It responded immediately, swelling and plumping up before his eyes.

Jeff grunted above him. He pushed his hips forward, the head of his dick brushing Tate's cheek. "Suck it."

Tate opened his mouth and allowed the cock to slip past his lips. The taste was amazing, sweet yet a little salty from sweat. Jeff's hands slid over his head, stopping at his shoulders and massaging roughly. Tate moved forward, taking the dick into his throat, moaning from the enjoyable pressure.

"Damn, Tate," Jeff whispered. "That feels so good."

Yes, it does, Tate thought as he bobbed on Jeff's prick. *God, what am I doing? This is going to fuck everything up.*

"Yeah, get that cock nice and hard, because it's going in your ass real soon." Jeff pulled his shirt off and tossed it aside. The streetlight sent just enough light through the trees to allow Tate to see his meaty frame. He was in shape, but not overly muscular. There was a sprinkling of hair on his chest and tummy. He looked just the way Tate had imagined.

Tate let the cock slip out of his mouth and looked up at his friend. "Who said anything about you fucking me?"

"I did." Jeff unbuttoned his pants and pulled them down. He kicked them and his sandals aside. "I want to and you're going to let me."

Hell, yes, I will. "I guess I could. You know, so you can experience it." He smiled. "Since you're curious."

"Right." Jeff put his hands on the back of Tate's head and pulled him toward his cock. "Suck me."

Shaking his head, Tate moved down to Jeff's balls. "You'll like this more." He licked them slowly, taking in the musky aroma of Jeff's crotch.

"Damn. You're right."

Tate let his tongue explore Jeff's body, moving slowly up the length of him. After stopping to tease his nipples for a few moments, he found himself face-to-face with his lover.

Jeff's grin returned. "You want to kiss me?"

"Yes."

"Okay." Jeff wrapped his arms around Tate and pulled him close.

Their lips collided and Tate felt his knees go weak. He had imagined this for so long and, now that it was actually happening, it was almost too much for him to handle. He ran a hand through Jeff's short blond hair, enjoying the softness.

Jeff's kiss was powerful. He may not have fucked many of those girls he had dated, but he sure had kissed them. That much was evident. No one becomes that good of a kisser without some practice.

Tate broke the kiss. "You're a good kisser."

"Thank you." Jeff ran his hands down Tate's back, shoving his hands into his back pockets and squeezing his ass tight. "You want to see how good of a fucker I am?"

Tate nodded.

"Good." Jeff moved his hands around to Tate's crotch, unbuttoning and unzipping in one swift motion. He pushed them down to the ground. "I don't think I can wait much longer."

Tate turned his back to his lover, pressing his ass against Jeff's throbbing dick. "Fuck me, Jeff." He had barely gotten the words out of his mouth when he found himself on all fours. Jeff helped him out of his sandals and pulled his shorts away.

"You ready?"

Looking over his shoulder, Tate saw Jeff spit into his hand then rub it on his cock. "Yes." He pressed his butt against the head of Jeff's manhood. "Fuck me."

Jeff pushed his meat forward against Tate's asshole, breaking past the tight knot of muscle and plunging deep.

Pain shot through Tate's abdomen and his head flew back. "Oh!"

"Does it hurt?" Jeff asked, already starting to pump.

"No," Tate lied. "It feels amazing. Oh, shit, Jeff, fuck me! Fuck me hard!"

Jeff did as requested, pounding Tate much more forcefully than he had ever been fucked.

Tate grit his teeth as his knees dug into the dirt. He grabbed his cock with one hand—using the other to hold himself up—and started jacking. "Damn, man."

"Your ass is so damn tight," Jeff whispered. "I'm about to blow my fucking load."

"Fill my ass," Tate demanded. "Fill my hole with your come!"

Jeff tightened his grasp on Tate's hips, slamming into him at an even faster pace. He kept the pace for a few more thrusts, but suddenly stopping moving. "Oh, shit!"

Heat filled Tate's asshole as Jeff released his seed. Tate let out an embarrassing scream as his own load shot from his cock, splattering on the dirt below him.

Jeff pulled his rod out of Tate's ass and collapsed on the ground, struggling to catch his breath. He reached out, pulling his lover on top of him. "That was fucking great."

"Yes, it was." Tate rested his head on Jeff's chest.

"I can't believe we just did that."

Tate exhaled slowly. "I know."

They rested in silence until Tate finally gathered the courage to ask what was on his mind. "Why did you want to try it with a guy?"

"Because."

"Because why?"

Jeff laughed, rolling onto his side and using one finger to tip Tate's face up to meet his own. "Because I've always wondered. And, you're gay, so I thought we—"

"Well, now you know." Tate interrupted. He sat up and reached for his shorts. "We need to get home."

Jeff took a hold of Tate's shoulder and pulled him back down. "Hey?"

"What?"

"We can chalk this up to us being drunk if you want."

Tate forced a smile, tying to hide his disappointment. *Of course it was just a fuck, idiot. He was just curious. And he used you . . .*

"But the next time we do it we'll both be sober." Jeff smiled.

"The next time?"

"Yeah." Jeff wrapped his hand around Tate's still erect cock, pumping it softly. "I mean, don't you want there to be a next time?"

Tate couldn't think of anything to say. All he could do was nod.

"Good." Jeff kissed Tate on the forehead. "That's what I wanted to hear."

A Pale Lover in the Moonlight

Joe Filippone

Tommy had noticed him the moment he walked into the frat house. The loud music rebounded off the walls with such force that the windows and picture frames rattled. The only way anyone could hold a conversation was if they were standing an inch away from someone's face and yelling at the top of their lungs. Even then, with the music raping their ears and ravishing their eardrums, it was still impossible to hear. But then, no one goes to frat parties to engage in deep conversation about Melville and Hemingway.

Tommy hated these parties. His frat house threw at least one a week, so it was required that he attend. If he could, he would have left and spent a quiet evening at the library or the movies. He had never been into parties, especially frat parties and all the events that went with it: drinking, drugs, and casual sex. Yes, Tommy was not the typical frat boy. He only drank on holidays and birthdays, and usually it was no more than one glass. He didn't do drugs, and in his nineteen years on earth he had only slept with one guy.

He had been all set to retreat upstairs to his room and seek refuge in sleep. Screw 'em if the other guys gave him shit for leaving the party early. He was bored; there was no one there worth talking to. Everyone was acting like a fool. Most of the guys in his frat house were running around naked. Most of the girls were nude as well. People were fucking right in the living, not caring who saw or who joined in. He shook his head and started to head upstairs when he saw him walk through the door.

Tommy nearly tripped and fell down the stairs when he saw him. This guy was really, *really* hot—the type of guy that made a flock of butterflies do out-of-control loop-de-loops in his stomach. The boy was short, probably no more than five-four, and thin as a rake. His hair, an emo-style cut, was a light gingerbread color with marigold yellow streaks. He was clad all in black: a tank top that showed off the cinnamon-colored hair under his arms and a pair of tight black jeans that showed off his nonexistent ass. Tommy's tongue flicked out and licked his lips. Damn! That guy was hella hot!

The frat boy stood on the steps frozen like a victim of Medusa. He wanted to go over and talk to the pale hottie, but he couldn't move. His legs felt like they were stuck in concrete. His heart pounded and he started to sweat because, despite his outward appearance and the confidence he exuded, Tommy was very, *very* scared of guys. Plus he was worried that the hottie was straight—he had walked in with a very pretty redhead. Tommy sighed. Why were all the hot guys either straight, crazy, or assholes?

Rion, the hottie who had caught Tommy's eye, followed his friend Lenore to the kitchen, or at least he tried. The frat house was so crowded that getting to the kitchen was like trying to get through an obstacle course. The small boy kept his head down, avoiding all eye contact. His stomach was twisted into a giant pretzel. Maybe this wasn't such a good idea.

He had never been to a party in his whole life and he never thought he would lose his party virginity at a frat house. He kept his gaze to the ground, scared to make eye contact with any of the muscular frat boys or beautiful girls.

"Don't look like you're being led to the firing squad," Lenore said, handing him a beer. "Look a little excited. This is a party."

A Pale Lover in the Moonlight

"I can't believe I let you talk me into this," Rion said, sipping his beer.

"Oh come on, Rion. College kids have to go to frat parties. It's in the Bible. Besides, if you didn't come tonight, what would you do? Stay in your dorm room and listen to that Swedish Death Metal you got a hard-on for?"

"I was planning to go to the movies tonight. The theatre's having a monster movie marathon."

"Rion, you are the most pathetic gay guy I've ever met. You don't party. You don't fuck around . . ." Lenore's voice tapered off.

"That's not my style. You know that."

"Then why go to college if you're not going to get drunk and fuck random people whose names you don't even know?" Lenore laughed and chugged her beer with an expertise that would make even the most hardcore alcoholic blush with shame.

"Call me a freak, but I enrolled in college to get an education so I don't spend the rest of my life working in a Wal-Mart like my folks."

"Freak." She smiled at him before belching and crushing the beer can into oblivion. "Come on, it's one party. Promise me you'll try to have fun. Don't go sitting on the couch all night."

"You're leaving me?" He panicked. Besides Lenore he didn't know anyone there.

"Yeah," she said as if it should have been obvious. "Have you seen all the hot guys here? It's going to be like fishing at one of those trout farms." She winked and walked away, seductively accentuating her hips and going on the hunt for hot frat boy sex.

Rion let out a sigh so big his shoulders rose up to his ears before heavily dropping. He looked around. Everyone was hooked up and having a great time. Except him. Looking around and making sure Lenore was out of sight, he walked over to the beer-stained sofa and sat down. Hopefully time would soar. He looked at his watch. Maybe he would sneak out. If he left now he could make it to the movie theatre before they started the monster marathon.

He looked around the room, trying to see if Lenore was in eyesight. He did not want to have to deal with her giving him shit for leaving early. He was thankful when he saw her walk up the stairs with the tight end of the football team. Rion strained his neck getting a better view of the football star; he really did have a tight end. Rion was a little jealous that Lenore would get to see the hot jock nude and find out if he was an MVP.

"Monster marathon, here I come," Rion said to himself, getting up and starting to walk toward the door.

Tommy had been making his way toward the couch where the skinny hottie sat. The girl he had walked in with had gone upstairs with Booker, the star tight end. The hottie looked miserable. Tommy smiled a little; maybe this was the opening he needed. He could sit down next to the guy and strike up a conversation with him—maybe make him feel better. He quickened his pace when he saw the hottie get up and make his way toward the door. Tommy was not going to let him get away.

"Hey." Tommy stopped in front of the guy and smiled.

"Hey." The boy's voice was minute and he avoided looking at Tommy.

"I'm Tommy." He extended his hand.

"Rion." He timidly took Tommy's hand. Tommy liked the way his smooth hand fit comfortably in Tommy's muscular palm.

"Nice to meet you. You leaving the party already?"

"Yeah." Rion's heart beat faster and he looked for an alternate escape route in case Tommy tried to prevent him from leaving. "No offense, but parties aren't really my thing."

"I understand. I'm not really a party boy myself."

Rion looked up, shocked. Tommy looked like the party boy of the world. He was tall and muscular, with sandy blond hair that fell to just above his shoulders. He exuded confidence from his pores. Rion was sure all he had to do was smile at the boy he wanted to fuck and the boy would gladly rip off his clothes and let Tommy fuck him wherever they were.

"So where are you heading?" Tommy asked.

"The movie theatre. They're having a monster movie marathon."

As soon as he got the words out, Rion felt his cheeks burn as embarrassment hit him full force with her whip. He knew he sounded like the world's biggest dork and was waiting for Tommy to laugh at him.

Much to Rion's surprise Tommy said "Cool. I love monster movies."

"Really?" Rion asked suspiciously, still not sure if this was a trick or not.

"Yeah. You wanna get outta here and go to the movies?"

"Sure." Rion smiled, happy for the company.

Tommy also smiled, glad that he was going to be alone with the boy. He was even hotter close up. His eyes were long and oblong and his skin was a pale tan color. Tommy guessed he probably had some Asian in him. Tommy had always liked Asian guys. He couldn't help staring at the way his armpit hair peeked out from his tank top. Tommy loved guys with armpit hair.

The two boys walked out of the frat house into the crisp autumn night. The smell of leaves crackly with age invaded their nostrils. The moon was a pale blue, shooting a large beam of lavender light to the world below. A warm breeze lightly caressed their skin.

"Nice night," Tommy said.

"Yeah," Rion said.

He liked Tommy. He seemed really nice. Real. Not like most frat boys who were only interested in alcohol and sex. He was also really, *really* hot, resembling one of those hotties on those dramas on the CW that Rion lusted and masturbated over.

The two boys arrived at the movie theatre with just over five minutes to spare before the marathon started. Tommy bought them a big tub of popcorn, a large Sierra Mist for them to share, and two boxes of malted milk balls. They walked into the theatre, filled to overflowing, and found two seats in the back row.

Tommy cheered when the lights dimmed and a huge fake-looking fifties sci-fi movie monster filled the screen. Rion laughed at the way Tommy was sitting on the edge of his seat, stuffing popcorn and malted milk balls into his mouth and staring wide-eyed at the screen like a little kid.

"Oh man. Look at that thing eat the city. This is so cool," Tommy gushed.

"You don't look like the type who would be into this stuff."

"Are you kidding? I'm president of the school's sci-fi club."

"The school has a sci-fi club?" Rion's body perked up.

"Yeah. It's really small right now and we've only had one meeting, but we're growing. You wanna join?"

"Sure," Rion said, excited. He had always been a sci-fi geek and was excited to be able to connect with fellow sci-fi geeks.

After the movie, the two boys took the long way back to the frat house via the park. Neither of them knew when it had happened, but they were holding hands. Tommy's fingers lightly caressed Rion's knuckles, sending little tingles up and down Rion's spine.

A Pale Lover in the Moonlight

"I had a really nice time tonight," Tommy said, drawing Rion close to him.

"Me, too."

"I was watching you," Tommy confessed. "When you first walked into the house. I thought you were pretty cute." Tommy's confession made Rion blush. "Although when I saw you with that girl I thought you were straight."

This last part made Rion laugh. No one had ever mistaken him for straight. If anything, Tommy was the one who could pass for straight.

"Lenore's just a friend."

"Yeah, I kind of figured that out when I saw her go upstairs with Booker."

Both of them laughed.

"I'm glad you came over and talked to me. I'm glad Lenore convinced me to go to the party."

"Same here," Tommy took Rion's face in his hands and gently leaned in and kissed him.

Rion's arms wrapped tightly around Tommy's neck. Tommy's hands snuck under Rion's T-shirt and lightly caressed his back. Their bodies were pressed against each other. They could feel each other's throbbing cocks, threatening to explode from their pants like ticking time bombs.

"The party should be over by now," Tommy said when their lips parted. "Do you want to go back to the house? Back to my house?"

Rion didn't know what came over him. He never thought he would sleep with a guy on the first date, let alone a guy he had only known for a few hours, but before he knew it he heard the words "I'd like that" pour over his lips.

Tommy smiled, put his arms around Rion, and drew him

close. The two continued walking back to the house. The anticipation of what was going to happen once they reached their destination made their steps increase to a quick trot.

The two exploded into Tommy's room, lips locked in a hard kiss. Their hands roamed each other's bodies. Tommy wasted no time in getting Rion out of his clothes. He pushed the smaller boy onto the bed, bathing his body in the soft moonlight that came in through the window.

"You are so fuckin' beautiful," Tommy said as he leaned down and gently kissed Rion's small nipples, the color of aged almonds. His hands roamed over the boy's smooth body.

Tommy snaked lower and lower down Rion's body. His tongue swiveled around his navel as he played with Rion's smooth kiwi-shaped balls. Taking Rion's swollen cock in his hand, he lightly caressed it over his lips before swallowing him whole. Rion's back arched and his body rippled with passion. His hands got lost in Tommy's hair, his legs wrapped around his shoulders, pushing Tommy's head down further and making him gag on his cock. Rion was sure he would come when Tommy swallowed his whole cock and licked his full balls.

Tommy had fumbled with his jeans, clumsily getting out of them before discarding his own shirt. His hard pecs glistened in the moonlight and his cock stood proudly at attention.

Sitting up, Rion sucked Tommy's cock like a lollipop, kissing the tip of his cock before licking the hard length up and down and then swallowing him whole. Rion's hands clutched Tommy's round ass, sticking a few fingers in his long, deep crack. Tommy threw his head back and grunted, digging his nails into Rion's shoulders. Tommy clutched Rion's shoulders and thrust his hips back and forth, fucking Rion's mouth at warp speed.

After a while, Tommy gently pushed Rion back onto the bed

and threw his legs over his shoulders. Grasping his cock in his fist, Tommy teased Rion's ass, slapping his cock against Rion's cheeks and rubbing it in his crack before pushing himself slowly into Rion, inch by inch. Rion trembled as Tommy's cock penetrated him. He could feel Tommy's cock pulsating with the blood of lust. Tommy ran his hands over Rion's body, pinching his hard nipples. Rion's own hands were gently pulling on Tommy's own large silver-dollar-sized nipples.

The two boys kept their gaze locked on each other as Tommy thrusted in and out of Rion's ass. Sweat oozed out of their pores. Tommy's balls were slapping hard against Rion's ass. The light of the moon kept its lavender spotlight on them, giving them an otherworldly hue.

Taking hold of Rion's arms, Tommy pulled Rion on top of him. Rion placed his hands on Tommy's chest to steady himself and rode Tommy's hard cock.

After a while, Rion decided to lift himself up until just the tip of Tommy's cock was inside his ass; then he would roughly impale himself on the hard length. Tommy slapped Rion's ass and bucked his hips up, penetrating him more. Tommy's fist was tightly holding Rion's cock, jerking him off in sync to his thrusting.

Tommy's face contorted into a mask of passion. He threw his head back, letting loose an animalistic growl, and his body arched when his come exploded into Rion's ass. A few seconds later, Rion's own come followed, staining Tommy's pink nipples the color of fresh milk.

Rion collapsed on top of Tommy, smearing his body with his own come. The two kissed. Tommy's cock was still embedded deep in Rion's ass, pulsing against him. Their hands roamed each other.

"That was great," Tommy said breathless.

"Yeah," Rion rolled off him.

"Um ... Do you maybe wanna spend the night?" Tommy didn't look Rion in the eye, fearing rejection.

"I'd like that," Rion said kissing him.

Tommy smiled and wrapped his arms tighter around Rion. He smiled up at the moon bathing them in its light, thankful that both of them had been at the party.

Break on Through

Simon Sheppard

He was an asshole. A handsome asshole with a big dick, but an asshole nonetheless. I first scoped him out in the locker room. I was there to shower after a particularly sweaty folk dance class. He was there because he was a big, butch jock. I noticed his six-pack, his broad shoulders, his big, uncut dick. I may be an overeducated hippie, yeah, but I notice these things.

He noticed me noticing. He didn't look away. His dick began to swell—slightly, but just enough—before he turned away and wrapped a towel around his waist. You gotta love it.

When I mentioned his name, as casually as possible, to my friend Becky, she confirmed what I thought I already knew about him. Business major. Frat rat. No doubt he'd voted for Nixon in the last election. "Why?" she asked slyly. "You interested in getting in his pants or something? Well, take heart. I always assume that anyone who's buttoned up so tight has something to hide."

Now, we all know—at least, most of us do—that there are jocks on campus who will, after a few beers or an unsatisfactory date, allow some gay guy to blow them . . . only to ignore them the next day, or worse, make fag jokes to their friends. I'm sorry, but no matter how horny I may get—and I get pretty goddamn horny—I've always found the whole thing kind of disgusting. Not that I'm the hardest-core gay-lib type, but I have no great desire to serve as a come dump for some macho moron who would just as soon spit on me as fuck me.

I understand why some gay guys might disagree. Even on a

campus as large as this one, there aren't that many guys who are out. When I finally got up the guts to go to a gay lib meeting, I discovered that most of the men there were townies, and not many of them, even. A small dating pool, or tricking pool, or whatever. So some guys are only too happy to take whatever dick they can find. Not me. I have too much self-respect for that.

Still, I did find it hard not to think of Brian's cock. And yes, the next time I saw him in the locker room and our eyes met, we both started getting hard. On the other hand, later, when I saw him walking arm-in-arm with his girlfriend, he didn't even look my way. Asshole, like I said.

So there I am late one night, coming down off acid, feeling vulnerable and, well, cosmically horny. It's about two a.m. and I'm all alone out in front of the Student Union, and wow, there's Brian. Part of me is still high enough to believe this was all meant to be, and a lot of me is still high enough to believe that when he comes over and says hi, he seems kind of sweet and easygoing, and not really an asshole at all. I do have to admit to myself, though, that the thought of his foreskin plays a part in my calculations.

He says "How you doing?" and I say "Not bad." I don't really want to get into how I've recently had a face-to-face with God and how things have just now stopped wavering around enough for me not to feel Technicolor nausea anymore. What I want to get into—qualms or no—is his pants.

I can, in fact, smell liquor on his breath, and while that's tactically a point in my favor, it also rings a warning bell, since drunk straight guys can be fucking dangerous, even when they're wanting to get blown. And Brian wants to get blown. I can see that; he's not keeping it much of a secret. He doesn't know how to tell me, though, how to ask. So he just sits there making inane small talk, while I want to let him know that it's all okay because the universe is really truly One, and that I like his foreskin, even though I think he's a dick.

One of the things that LSD has taught me is that we're all living out these narratives that we've invented, even if we're totally unaware we're doing that. He's part of my story, I'm part of his, and because of who he is and who I am, at the moment I have—whatever it might look like—the upper hand. I think that's because, to get what we both want, he has to be willfully stupid. I don't.

So we talk for a while, and I can almost see the words ballooning out of his mouth in a little alcoholic haze, and then I say that I'm kind of tired and cold and I want to go back to my room and listen to music and does he want to come along.

I'm glad—not for the first time—that I managed to swing a single room from Campus Housing. It's late enough so not many people will be in the hallways of the dorm, and those who are might think that Brian's a secret stoner who's going to cop dope from me. Becky would know what was really going on, of course, but Becky won't be there.

So we head back to my dorm as though we're in some archetypal story or other, and though I'm understanding how complex all this is, I'm also enjoying the closeness of Brian, and that surprises me. But the day has been full of surprises, so what the hell.

When we get back to my dorm room, I light a stick of incense, put a towel against the crack at the bottom of the door, and start to roll a joint. Brian right away sprawls himself on the bed, legs spread, crotch pointed toward me like he's some slut from *Hustler*. Straight guys.

I put on The Byrds—I've just gotten a new copy of *Fifth Dimension* to replace the one that got ruined by candle wax—light the joint, take a deep hit, and hand it over to him, ready to tell him what to do with it. But that's not necessary. It's evident that he's smoked dope before, which makes me wonder how he can be what he is. Anyway, we pass the joint back and forth a few times, till I've gotten what I needed and Brian looks like he's stoned, too.

We sit around for a few minutes, sort of drifting aimlessly. Brian's making his intentions pretty clear: His hand keeps drifting down toward his crotch. Except I've got the karmic drop on him. I know what's going to happen. He doesn't.

The Byrds aren't the right soundtrack, not for this. I put on the Doors' first album instead. Jim Morrison in leather pants, yeah. I can see Brian's got a boner hidden in his pants. And I know he wants me to desire him, to service him, to make his straight dick come. But like I said, I know what's going to happen. I stand up in front of the bed, dead center between his spread legs.

I smile. He smiles back, nervously.

"Get down on your knees," I say.

"Huh?" he says.

"On your knees."

He starts to unbutton his shirt. I know he wants to show me what he's got, make me desire him. That will give him power. No dice. "Keep your clothes on," I say, my voice hardly raised at all, not trembling. "All of them."

He stops fiddling with the buttons.

"And get down on your knees."

I'm not really surprised at all that he does. Get down.

He looks up at me like he's on the wrong end of a telescope. "You want me to suck your dick?" he asks.

"Yeah, I want you to suck my dick."

The Doors are thrashing away. I'd turn up the phonograph, but it's late and I don't want to wake up my neighbors. The fewer interruptions, the better.

I'm stripping naked. "Just think of it like a hazing."

He doesn't say a thing. I stand in front of him and run my hands all over my hairy, skinny body, like I'm the hot one, not him. My cock is so hard it almost hurts.

He's on his knees, staring up at me. He makes a grab for his crotch.

"Hands off," I say. It's *my* narrative, *my* story. He's just a character.

Then he says something weird. "Don't hurt me," he whimpers.

Until that moment, the thought had never crossed my mind. Now I'm suddenly furious. At least *somebody's* furious, maybe someone a long ways away.

"Open your fucking mouth." I'm not in any doubt.

And he does it.

I put the wet head of my cock up against his mostly closed lips. Brian might have smoked dope before, but it seems clear he hasn't ever sucked cock. I make things explicit, anyway. "You ever suck dick before?"

He shakes his head no.

"You sure?"

"Sure."

Well, even if he's lying, I fucking don't care. "Kiss it," I say.

He gives my dick a little peck, an auntie's kiss.

"Kiss it like you mean it."

He opens his lips. I can feel his tongue on my cockhead.

"Now take the head of my dick in your mouth. Just the head."

He does it, because . . . because that's precisely what he's meant to do.

"Nurse on it."

He sucks a bit, kind of tentatively.

"Yeah, fratboy, just like that."

He reaches down for his crotch again.

"I said hands off." His hand comes away.

The tip of my dick is still in his mouth. His breathing is coming quicker now. The acid hasn't entirely worn off; I'm feeling really, really stoned.

"Now take the rest of my dick in your mouth." He slides his lips halfway down the shaft. "And watch your teeth."

He stops, backing off my cock. I'm afraid for a second that he's changed his mind. But no, he pauses, then sticks out his tongue and begins to lick the underside of my shaft.

"Good," I say, "good."

Brian looks pleased, then gulps down my whole dick. He obviously isn't ready for that; he begins to gag.

I slide my cock halfway out of his throat. "Relax," I say. "Breathe. A little bit of cock isn't going to kill you." He collects himself, gets over the gagging, relaxes. And I slam my dick all the way down his throat. He sputters, looks surprised. I grab the back of his short-haired head and fuck his throat. I can see he's getting the dry heaves.

"Look at me." He looks up, my dick still in his mouth. Tears are in his eyes.

You remember how Oppenheimer said, when the first atomic bomb went off, "Now I am become Shiva, destroyer of worlds?" Well, I have become Shiva, destroyer of straight boys.

"You're not going to puke, got it?"

He nods.

"Even when I shoot down your throat."

The needle lifts off side one of the Doors album. I'm not about to go turn it over.

"So go on and suck it, asshole."

It's just pure pleasure to look down and see the straight boy servicing my dick, making me feel good. Taking it.

Break on Through

Brian is an okay cocksucker. Nothing spectacular, but not bad for a first-timer. I figure he's maybe picked up some pointers from the girls who've gone down on him. I'm wishing they could see him now. Drool is running down his chin.

For a minute, I think about fucking him as well, but I've bottomed enough times to know that he might well enjoy it. And I don't want that.

Brian is starting to shift from knee to knee, obviously getting uncomfortable. And I've had a really long day. Much as I may want this to go on till dawn, I figure it might be just as well to let him have it. I reach up and pinch my nipples.

"Oh yeah," I say, "I'm gonna shoot a fuckload in your straight-boy mouth. Fratboy cocksucker."

He moans and sucks harder, and that does it. I tense my ass, shove my cock as far down Brian's throat as I can, and come. It's one of those multicolored LSD orgasms, and it lasts forever. And ever. Actually, I hate to admit it, but it's one of the very best orgasms of my life.

When I finally stop pumping out jism, I pull my dick out of Brian's mouth. It would be hot if there were a trickle of come running down his chin, but you can't have everything.

Brian looks stoned and confused.

"You want to come?" I ask.

He nods.

"Okay, whip it out and jack off. You have my permission."

He looks up at me, my dick in his face, as he unzips his pants. He pulls out his dick, which is large as I remember and—to the surprise of neither of us—hard. He slides his generous foreskin back and forth over his damp dickhead.

"I'm going to come. That okay?"

He's asking permission. *That's hot.*

"Yeah," I say. "Go on ahead."

He's looking up at me like he's suddenly in love with me, which is sort of creepy for some reason. "Fuck," he says. He sprays a big load of come, gob after gob, all over my rug.

"You've made a mess," I say. "Lick it up."

"Really?" he says, like it's the first thing tonight that he can't believe.

"We've come this far," I say. "Lick it up and you can leave."

He hesitates for a second, looking up at me, then bends over and slurps his come from my rug.

He suddenly bolts back on his haunches, struggles to his feet, runs over to the sink in the corner of my room, dick still sticking out of his pants, and vomits. It's not exactly the perfect end to a perfect evening, but it will have to do. When he's done, he rinses out the sink, puts his cock away, and turns to go. He's at my door when he turns. "Thanks," he says. Thanks.

I lock the door after him, and put the Byrds back on, then light another stick of incense to get the smell of puke out of the air.

I take a hit off the roach, and lie back on the bed. I figure that this will never happen again, that when I see Brian again, maybe with some girlfriend, he won't even look my way. That's fine. As long as he doesn't yell shit at me at some antiwar demonstration, I'll keep our little cosmic secret. And maybe in some future, when today is a vague, muddled, and possibly mythic memory, he'll be some executive somewhere and I'll be an artist and I'll be demonstrating against his stupid corporation profiting from some other stupid war. Or maybe—more improbable things have happened, I guess—it will be vice versa, and I'll be the one with a briefcase and he'll be the one with the picket sign. I realize with a stoned little shock that I fucking have no idea. All I know for sure is that I have been, for one long instant, Shiva. With a hard-on. Destroyer of straight boys. Sure thing.

I turn off the light, lie there listening to the comfortingly cosmic sounds of The Byrds, wait for things behind my eyelids to stop spinning so much, and then drift off into what I fully expect to be an untroubled sleep.

Peanut Butter and Jelly

Marcus James

For my own Max Evans (Are you in, or are you out?)

Have you ever met someone who you knew in the first five seconds of laying eyes on them that you were destined to know each other for the rest of your lives? Have you ever looked into a person's eyes and seen your own endlessness reflect in them, experienced those eyes swallowing you whole and making you forget everything that you could possibly feel is wrong with you? It doesn't happen very often; in fact, the possibility of it occurring is mostly slim to none, but if you are lucky enough to have it happen then you know that you'll never be the same again.

It happened to me. The funny thing is I thought it never would. I relegated those things to television and the next thing I know I'm in the middle of my own personal sitcom, my own silver screen script. If this were *Roswell* (my favorite show) I'd be Liz Parker minding my own business at the Crashdown Café and he'd be my own Max Evans coming to look right into me and touch my very soul.

All of these stories have a beginning: a place where the tale kicks off and, as with all stories, the ending always comes with monumental revelations. My story, this story that you're reading, is no different.

I was sitting in my English class at Atherton University, a private Ivy League college on the east coast, a college full of bloodlines and bank accounts, and my life was no exception. When your life is a guarantee it's pretty hard to fuck it up, but if you're gay that can seriously throw a monkey wrench into the whole thing. I wanted my mother to be proud of me; despite generations of living at the same address, my family had always been considered the black sheep of the Upper East Side and my mother had felt that if anyone had the chance to turn that around it was going to be me. But then I came out of the closet and my family felt that I had thrown our path off course.

I made a deal with them then. I wouldn't date anyone while at Atherton. I would not make us the product of another scandal if it could be helped. But then I dared to look around the classroom and allow my eyes to wander to the faces around me. This was, of course, something I never did, namely because I knew that wandering eyes breed temptation. Even though I was lonely and wished desperately to be with someone, someone who could— no, would—know me inside and out, I knew that, to quote Frost, I had promises to keep and miles to go before I sleep.

I should have known what was coming. I should have anticipated its tremors, but it seems like with all things, I am blissfully unaware of everything around me. I searched the room and the class consisted of nameless, faceless masses paying attention to what the professor was talking about. Thus, the only thing I could spy was the backs of their heads. I looked back down at my notes and rapped the back of my pen on the two-sizes-too-small folding desk attached to the side of my seat. I thought that perhaps this had been for the best: I had been saved. But then, as if I had spoken too soon, I felt the sensation of eyes burning into me. When I cocked my head, my eyes met with another's.

They were big and brown—not the kind of brown that everyone has, but that dark Latin brown that looks closer to black. They seemed luminous and the lights of the room reflected and danced on them as if they were water. He had a very strong and distinct jaw, a smooth face, and soft caramel skin. His hair was black and fashioned in a hip faux-hawk; I could tell that he probably spent two hours on his hair every morning. Now normally I would find this appalling, but for some reason with him I found it to be instantly endearing. He had bulky arms and broad shoulders, but the kindness in his eyes seemed to calm my nerves and make me forget where I even was at that moment.

I glimpsed his black tee and saw Greek letters printed on the left breast; it was a shirt for Sigma Gamma Phi. I knew that house; it was the most sought-after frat house on campus. My father and forefathers had all been legacies; I was so glad my father had passed away for that reason alone. No pressure to pledge, and no reason to try and be something I wasn't.

Class ended and he stood, grabbing his peacoat and heading out the door. I had never taken my coat off, and yes, just as with every east coaster, I was also wearing one. I wanted to catch up with him, talk to him or something, but he was gone in a sea of students and I made my way to my next class.

"So there's a party tonight. You going?" I looked at my roommate Nathaniel Van Tassel and shook my head. Like me, Nathaniel was part of the silver spoon club of the Upper East Side. In fact, we had both attended St. John's Academy together, though we had never been friends. When we learned, to our shock and mild amusement, that not only were we both at Atherton, but that we were roommates, we learned to get along.

"No."

"Why not?"

I sighed before responding. "Because you know how I get at

those things. I stand against a wall nursing a couple of drinks, stumble through awkward conversations, and then leave before you do, stealing a bottle of vodka and sneaking it back into the room."

He ran his hand through his sandy hair and laughed. "Yeah, that's true, but this will be different. I promise."

"Where's it at?" I could feel my stomach turning in knots; I could feel what was going to come out of his mouth.

"It's at Sigma Gamma Phi." Yeah, I was definitely going now.

Sigma Gamma Phi was housed in a pristine three-story brownstone on the edge of campus with English lattice frames and dim lighting. We walked in, shuffling through the crowds, and all I wanted to do was find the boy from my English class. I was wearing black and gray plaid slacks and a ribbed V-neck sweater with the usual white collared shirt and a Burberry tie. I felt good; I felt that this had been an appropriate choice for an outfit to wear when trying to catch the eye of a guy, and once more, I felt confident, which was a rarity for me.

I grabbed a plastic cup filled with some alcoholic punch that seemed electric red and searched the room, eagerly looking for that hair and those eyes. It didn't take me very long to find my target. He was standing against the stone mantle of the fireplace, not talking to anyone, and expressing a boredom that was familiar to me. It was the same kind of detachment that I myself always seemed to possess at these things. I took a deep breath and walked up to him, feeling as if everything was parting to make way for me, as if it were destiny.

He looked at me and smiled. I returned it casually, then dared to speak.

"So most guys buy their underwear a size smaller than they actually wear to enhance the size of their packages. Do you do that?"

He grinned and looked down at his crotch for a moment, and still holding that grin, he looked back at me.

"Sometimes." At that very second I knew he was the one. "What about you?"

I shook my head. "No. I wear a size small. If I did that I would have to wear boys' underwear. Oh, and I wear briefs."

He smiled playfully. "Good to know."

We watched a girl walk by with too much eye shadow, come-fuck-me heels, and a three-sizes-too-small strapless dress. I felt my usual response creep up out of my throat. At the same time I could see this happening with the guy whose name I still did not know, and in unison we said:

"Tranny mess!" We looked at one another, dropped our jaws, and then laughed.

"That was so fetch!" he said. I nodded and laughed.

"Super fetch betch!" It was perfect, it was amazing, and I was glowing inside—just lighting up and feeling my heart warm.

"I'm Mattie," he said. I shook his hand and it seemed as if this kinetic surge passed between us. "Marcos," I responded.

We began talking about everything, things that had no point really, but things nonetheless that mattered to us.

"So, can I get a number?" I nodded and waited for him to pull out his cell phone, which he never did.

"Where's your phone?" I asked. He shook his head and smiled.

"I don't have a cell phone anymore—just a phone in my room." I pulled out my phone, feeling as if I had the upper hand.

"Then why don't you give me your number?"

"Okay." He told me his digits and I said goodnight. I walked away without looking back. I wasn't going to turn around, even though I really wanted to. Even though it was eating at me to whip my head around and take one last look, I knew I couldn't. It's so much cooler when you don't look back.

"Where did you go?" Nathaniel asked me when he walked back into the room, pulling off his scarf and jacket.

"I came back home."

He sighed and kicked off his shoes. "I know, why?"

I wasn't sure if I should tell him that I got a number, because this would only enforce his ego. The truth of it was, though, I wanted to tell someone. I wanted to tell the entire world that Marcos Bastille met a guy!

"C'mon, what happened? Do I need to kick someone's ass?"

I grinned and touched my cell, which was sitting on the bed next to my thigh. "I met a guy."

Nathaniel smiled. His smile was saying *I told you so.* I wanted to kick in his nuts for that.

"So, who is the lucky bastard?" It had never occurred to me that perhaps Mattie was lucky enough to have met me. The truth is, I always see myself as the fortunate one, the one who caught the prize. The idea of me being the prize was a completely alien concept.

"Um, Mattie. He's a brother . . ." I mumbled the last bit of information.

"A what?"

I shook my head and rolled my eyes, knowing that he had heard it. He only wanted to hear me say it aloud. "A brother, all right? He's a brother at Sigma Gamma Phi." I anticipated his smart-ass laugh and, sure enough, I got it. I have heard that laugh of his throughout most of my life—in the halls and in seats behind me and beyond me in classes. It was never a malicious laugh, just annoying, but it was part of who Nathaniel Van Tassel was, and you couldn't take one without the other.

Peanut Butter and Jelly

"Do you think his frat brothers know?" I hadn't even thought about this before; the question of whether or not Mattie was out hadn't even crossed my mind. But how could they not know? It wasn't like it was hard to figure out.

"Well, I'm not going to think about that right now. If anything, I'll find out if we ever even talk again . . ." My words trailed off at the end and I was trying to shrug off the uncertainty in my voice.

"Why do you say that?"

I wasn't sure why I had said it, but that's how I felt about the situation; maybe it was my insecurity in dating, because dating was something that I never did. I'd had private school encounters with a couple of guys, but I'd only had sex twice, and neither of those came from relationships. But that was the old me; that was pre-Atherton and promises to my mother. Now I was here and for the first time I had the chance to pursue something that I had always desired, the one thing I craved above all else: a real relationship with another guy.

"Call him." Nathaniel's words drew me back, away from my cyclone of thoughts, and I raised my eyebrow with a questioning look. "If you have his number you should call him. I mean the party's over now so I'm sure he's sitting on his bed with bated breath staring at his phone, waiting for you to call so he can catch it at the first ring."

He looked away from me awkwardly.

"And how would you know this?"

He shrugged. "Don't take this to mean I'm hitting on you or anything, but if it were me waiting for you to call, I'd be doing the same thing." And with that he grabbed his towel and walked into the bathroom. I waited till the door latched and the lock clicked before pulling up Mattie's number and giving him a call.

"Hello?"

My mind suddenly went blank.

"Is uh—" Shit! I was losing it. "Is Matt-Mattie there?" I felt relieved to hear him chuckle.

"Fuck yeah!"

I felt comfortable enough to laugh, and laughing felt exceptionally good at that moment.

"Oh, good. So what's going on?" I knew that this was a totally lame question, but I felt that it was a tried and true tool at starting a conversation.

"Nothing. I'm about to head to the gym, but I knew that I had to wait and talk to you first. I mean, I would look totally shitty if I didn't answer the phone when you called. You'd think I really didn't want to talk to you or something."

I was already smiling, a big smile that hurt my face. It was the kind of smile that you rarely suffer after the age of thirteen or so, after you find out the truth about Santa Claus, which then ruins the whole magic of Christmas.

"Yeah, I'd totally hate you." He laughed and we continued to talk for another fifteen minutes. He told me about how he wanted a little pig and he was surprised to learn that I also wanted one. As we talked I could not help but imagine what it would be like to sit next to him, to feel our arms touch, our hands clasp and fingers entwine. I thought about the magic of those eyes of his and how I could just fall into them, and what it would be like to feel his words emerge from his mouth, passing the moistness of his lips and slipping into my ear. The heat of his breath, the slight dampness of his speech, and I found my hand trailing down my stomach, moving over the bulge that was growing inside of my pants.

I kept one ear focused on the bathroom, relieved to hear the shower water running, and then I focused the rest of my attentions on not being found out by Mattie. I stroked the top of my cock and slapped it slightly before slipping my hand into my pants and underneath the hem of my briefs. I wrapped my fingers around the warmth of my stiff, growing cock and imagined that it was Mattie's hand and not mine that was in control. All the while I kept up my end of the conversation like a pro, like a CIA agent not letting on that he's wiretapping the entire conversation.

Mattie's voice was light, magical, but hinting at a deeper, much more sexually aware being that was desperate to come out. Perhaps he too was masturbating to this conversation and was attempting to hide it just as I was.

Between every *yes*, every *uh-huh*, I was pumping my shaft, feeling it rise up, feeling it get firmer and firmer, until I could feel those waves, that toe-curling, erratically thrilling sensation of orgasm ride up my legs and through my thighs before erupting out of my cockhead in a great rush, and I had to bite down on my lip to prevent myself from screaming out in pleasure.

I moved my pillow over my lap to cover the stain and it was then that our conversation was coming to a close, both of us agreeing to meet for lunch. I had thought it best that we meet up, but Mattie insisted on picking me up like a perfect gentleman, and who was I to argue with that?

The first date, and the many dates to follow, were the most amazing events of my life. And with Mattie they were always an event, even if it was simply the two of us sitting in his room or mine watching all of the *Scream* movies and making fun of them left and right. We incorporated lines from those movies, as well as *Cruel Intentions* and *Hocus Pocus*, into our daily vocabulary. We smoked pot, got drunk, and found things to be even better than they were sober.

We were taking things slow, which I liked, though often it

seemed as if we were moving at a snail's pace. But the truth of it is, and what I was learning, was that this better for us, especially since it was building the foundations of something very solid between us. Maybe more important, there were things about Mattie that he was afraid to let me see, things that he didn't want to expose me to because perhaps he thought that it would scare me away from him; but in the end, he was learning that there wasn't much he couldn't show me that I wouldn't be able to take. Perhaps it was because of how I grew up—in my world, you have to learn to look cheerful while under the table you're shoving a fork into the back of your hand.

Thanksgiving arrived sooner than I could have anticipated and Mattie expressed to me how he wasn't going to be able to go home for the holiday because his parents were out of the country doing outreach work. I offered for him to come join me for the holidays. The truth was, I didn't want to go home, but if I had to go, I wanted to show him off in front of my mother and everyone else in my family. I wanted to show them that I wasn't going to be their pawn anymore. I left Park Avenue and I wasn't going to be governed by its rules or theirs any longer.

We took the train. It wasn't a long journey, just a few hours, and when we arrived into Penn Station I could feel my heart beating erratically within my chest. I held Mattie's arm tightly, reluctant to let go for fear of falling under the weight of my own emotional baggage.

My mother's driver was waiting for us, and I could see by the look on Mattie's face that he wasn't used to Lincoln Town Cars and silent men in black suits and formal caps.

"Are you sure about this?" I asked him. He looked over at me and grinned. His neck was wrapped in a black and white checkered scarf and the bulk of his chest was evident through his black polo. I had casually mentioned that my mother was a fan of the polo; she had dressed me in them for years, and I must admit that out of habit or sheer liking for the style, I found myself wearing polos almost every day.

"I'm so sure." He leaned over and kissed my cheek. I blushed and smiled. "You know," he began, glancing down at my hand, which was entwined with his. "It makes me smile to see that I make you smile." At that I melted and smiled again.

"We don't have to do this. We can go back to the station if you want and we can spend Thanksgiving on campus."

He laughed and shook his head. "No way!"

I frowned.

"We can't," he said.

"Why not?"

"Because," he said calmly, looking towards the window. "We're here." He was right. The car had stopped and I hadn't even realized it. The driver walked over and opened the door, allowing us to step out and proceed as he went to the trunk to grab our luggage. I led Mattie to the front door of our four-story townhouse; I wasn't sure what to expect on the other side. It was the evening before the holiday and I didn't know if we were having a pre-party party, or if there were relatives already here, sleeping in guest rooms and waiting in the wings to criticize everything about my life. I pulled out my house key and opened the door, following up with a shout into the large hardwood foyer that we had arrived.

My mother came cascading down the spiral staircase in a blur of velvet and cashmere, her blonde hair pulled back from her face and her icy eyes catching the cool autumn light. She stared at me, allowing her mouth to attempt a smile, and then I watched her eyes widen and freeze on Mattie.

"Welcome to my home." She held her hand out to him. "I'm Jennifer Bastille, and you must be Mattie." He nodded and shook her hand.

"I'm glad to meet you. Marcos has told me so much about you." She offered a snide grin and directed it swiftly to me.

"Too bad I can't say the same, but then that's my son—always full of secrets." I averted my gaze and stared at my feet. Sensing my discomfort, Mattie reached out and took hold of my hand.

"Touché, Mother."

"Why don't you boys get settled and join me for dinner. Your brothers and everyone else will be here tomorrow. For tonight, though, it will be just the three of us." I nodded and led Mattie up the stairs. I really didn't want to be here, but I was grateful for the fact that he was with me.

"So, what is it that you like about my son?"

I looked at her from across the table and snarled. "Mom!" I hissed.

"What? I'm simply curious. I mean, you've never brought a boy home before, that's all." Mattie slipped his hand under the table and squeezed my thigh. I looked at him—those dark eyes, that stylish black hair, which he wore down for me, and his black Gucci glasses that he had slipped on after our nap, deciding against putting his contacts back in.

"It's okay, babes, I promise." He turned his attentions back to my mother just as the maid, Babette, removed the soup bowls. "I like him because he's sweet, because he's always remembering things for me that I can't. But most of all, he reminds me of how special I am, and how special I make him feel. I like that I can do that to someone. He's a romantic."

My mother laughed and picked up her second glass of merlot. "Isn't that the truth? A hopeless romantic, really. I swear Catholic school put too much virtue into my son. Despite the fact that he's had sex, you'd never know it; it's like he's still a virgin."

Peanut Butter and Jelly

"MOTHER!"

She looked at me and lifted her glass in a mock toast. "Oh it's true; you know it is, in fact." She allowed her eyes to once again wander over Mattie. "I'm almost certain that it's your virtue that attracted Mattie to you in the first place." I looked at him and watched as his eyes fell away from me and over to the plates that Babette was setting down before us. I knew that the rest of dinner would be swallowed up by the deafening sound of our silences.

"So, that was intense . . ." Mattie said to me as we lay in my bed; The curtains were drawn open and the glittering lights of the city came filtering in through the glass, bathing my shadow-black walls in splotches of white.

"I know," I hesitated on what I was going to say next, but I did it anyways. "About what she said—"

"She was right, you know . . ." I looked over at him, trying to decipher his eyes in the dark, but I couldn't. "Your innocence was much of my attraction to you . . . your virtue, as she put it." He had suddenly taken on a darker tone and it thrilled me and frightened me all at once.

"What do you mean by that?"

"If I had wanted to I could have seduced you, bedded you, and then I would have been done with you in the morning." An eerie truth seemed to linger then, and yet I wanted him to go on. I wanted to explore this darker note; I wanted to explore its primal meaning.

"You think it would have been so easy—many guys have tried and all have failed." I said this with the confidence of its truth; what I did not anticipate was his counter-truth, the sheer cunning and conviction of his sexual appeal.

"I would have known how to do it; I would have known how to conquer you." His words sent a chill down my spine and raised goose bumps across my flesh.

"And how would you have done it?" I reached out for him, stretching my arm across his bare chest. What I loved best was the warmth of Mattie's flesh, in contrast to my own, which always seemed to be cold.

"That's not important; don't worry about it. That's not what you were to me, so there's no reason to think about it, no reason to talk about it." I didn't like how he was brushing off the whole subject.

"But I want to know. Maybe I need to know." He grew quiet for a moment. It was as if I could feel the change in the air, a kind of distance that was growing between us, spacing us in a gulf made of my mattress and warmed by my comforter.

"No. Let's not talk about it. It doesn't matter because I love you." I froze at this. I had wondered when we were going to say it.

"I love you, too." That was it. We quit talking, closed our eyes, and went to sleep, wrapped in one another, legs entwined and arms draped around one another lazily.

Morning came and went, and by dinnertime everyone was over. My aunts, uncles, grandparents, friends of the family, and my brothers; the two of them too busy horsing around to care about anything.

"So, Mattie, what are you doing at Atherton?" my Aunt Abigail asked, sipping on her wine.

"I'm majoring in architecture and I am a member of Sigma Gamma Phi." My family seemed to perk up at this and I shrunk my head into my shoulders.

"Really? Marcos's father and grandfather and his father were all brothers; it was a shame that Marcos never pledged," my mother chimed in, looking at me and raising her glass. I returned her toast halfheartedly.

"Well, I like that he didn't. I couldn't see myself with another brother." I loved that he had said that, and to see that he was holding his own against my mother, and standing up for me as well. The rest of the night moved slowly, and eventually Mattie and I stole a bottle of wine and snuck up to my room, leaving everyone downstairs.

"That was so hot!" I said to him, leaning over and kissing his lips, tasting the fermented grapes on his mouth, breathing in the hot moistness of him. I loved the scent of his Old Spice deodorant, and whether it was that, the alcohol, or because I was ready, I moved in on him, attacking his mouth with my tongue and searching his body with my hands.

"Are you sure?" he asked me and I nodded with a drunken grin. I felt his hands exploring me, and my cock became painfully hard, threatening to burst the seams of my slacks. I moved my hands down to his crotch and felt his own hard-on eager to get free; and I was more than willing to assist in the matter.

We pulled our shirts off and I began trailing my tongue down his neck and shoulders, tasting the salt of his flesh. Then I made my way to his nipples, teasing them with my tongue, feeling them become erect between my teeth. I felt his body recoil and heard the shudder of excitement erupt from his throat.

I slipped down his stomach and reached for his belt buckle, which I undid furiously, followed by his slacks. I slipped them off and stared at him in his black and gray striped briefs. His stiff cock hit against me and I went down on it, sucking on it through the cotton of his briefs for just a moment before slipping those off as well and taking in the glory of his cock.

I grinned at him and then put it in my mouth, feeling his cockhead swell, his hips grinding gently as I ran my tongue along the shaft. Then I spent some time on his balls, allowing those orbs to sit in my mouth as I rolled my tongue around them. His hands sifted through my hair as I sucked him off. I felt him swell and I pulled my mouth off just as he shot his load all over my face. I bent down and placed my lips back on his cock, hearing him shudder as I sucked the pearly mess off of his dick and drank it down.

He laughed and flipped me over, making his way down to my dick, doing everything that I was doing, but with his own personal touches. He slipped his fingers between the crack of my ass and began fingering me as he sucked me harder and harder, forcing me to spill in his mouth.

I thought perhaps that he was going to fuck me, which I was used to, but it surprised me when he pulled out the lubricated condom and slipped it on my already-slick dick. I smiled and arched his legs over my shoulders and then I slipped into him, feeling the muscle fight against me for just a moment before he relaxed it and allowed me to move all the way in.

I fucked him then. I fucked him hard. Pumping and bucking against him, moving down hastily and kissing him feverishly. It felt good to be in his ass, to see him grip his own cock and start pumping it, matching the speed of my thrusts. We were feeling something great pass between us, and with our eyes both of us were expressing relief that we had waited. It made it so much stronger.

We fucked strong and hard, me moving in and out of his tight hole. Then, as if on cue, like in a movie, we shot our loads at the same time, Mattie shooting all over his chest and me spilling into the condom.

I thought we were done, even as we lay there an hour later. But then Mattie climbed back on top of me and began kissing me and stroking my dick again. Then, as if feeling the need to dominate me, he slipped another condom on his dick and moved down onto me, turning me over on my stomach and shoving himself inside gently. I reached up but he forced my arms down and held tight to my wrists, fucking me with a primal lust I had never experienced before. There was a need in him, a desire to explore me, to own me, to have me claimed as his and his alone. He made me shoot my load without having to do anything to my dick with his hands or my own. The light from the hall spilled on my face in a thin sliver and I looked to see my mother there, watching for just a second and grinning. I thought I would have stopped it, perhaps freaked out, but I didn't. I kept going and Mattie kept going, fucking me until it seemed the sun would come up and ruin it all.

The next day my mother gave me a lecture about creating a scandal, about doing things I had said I wouldn't. But then she expressed happiness in the fact that at least I had found someone who saw me as his passion rather than simply seeing something about me that he felt he could take away.

It's a year later now, and we're still together. We've talked about one day having children, and where we want to live after school. We're thinking about moving to Spain or Italy for a while. His frat brothers all know me and like me, and Nathaniel and Mattie have really taken to one another. Things have been good and will always be good—but then again, we both knew it, from the moment we first laid eyes on one another. Like peanut butter and jelly, we just fit.

The Basement

Stephen Osborne

His palms were sweaty. Jeremy hoped and prayed that no one would notice. He tried to keep his breathing steady. *Look him right in the eye,* he told himself. *Don't let him know how nervous you are.* Jeremy was thankful he was standing. If he'd been sitting, the jitters would infest his legs and they'd be bouncing uncontrollably.

Mick's stare bored into Jeremy. "Scared, Pledge?" Mick refused to use names. You didn't get called by your name by Mick until you were accepted as a Delt. The look he was giving Jeremy made it plain that Mick thought that eventuality unlikely.

"No, sir," Jeremy lied. He willed his eyes not to give him away.

Mick gave a slight nod and turned his attention to Tony, who was standing stiff as a board next to Jeremy. "How about you, Pledge? Are you scared?"

"No, sir."

"Then you're idiots." Mick allowed himself a slight smile. He began to pace in front of Jeremy and Tony, his hands behind his back like he was a general about to send his troops into battle. The smile vanished and his face hardened again. "What have you heard about the basement of this house?"

Jeremy frowned, uncertain if he should answer. Before he could, Tony spoke up. "You mean about the ghost, sir?"

Mick glowered. "No, I'm referring to the crickets that hide out down there in the summer. Of course I mean the ghost! What do you know about the ghost, Pledge?"

Since Mick wasn't looking at either of them, Jeremy wasn't sure if he should answer. When Tony remained silent, he piped up with, "Supposedly, the ghost of a football player who was a Delt back in the seventies haunts the basement. He committed suicide down there, sir."

"Supposedly?" Mick raised his eyebrows. "I take it that you don't believe in ghosts, Pledge?"

Jeremy wasn't sure how he was supposed to answer, so he stammered a little. "I'm not . . . that is, I don't think . . . I like to keep an open mind about such things, sir."

Mick seemed satisfied with the response. He turned back to Tony. "What about you, Pledge? What do you think?"

Tony couldn't help the small smile that crept over his features as he said, "I ain't afraid of no ghosts, sir." He mimicked, rather closely, Ray Parker Jr's tone in the *Ghostbusters* theme.

Mick nodded. "Normally, I would agree with you, Pledge. Most ghost stories are just that. Stories. Tales told to scare people at Halloween. This one is different, though." Mick paused and ceased pacing as he bit his lip in thought. "This one is very different. I know I don't like to go down to the basement. Not by myself at night, certainly." He spoke as if he were talking to himself, as if Tony and Jeremy weren't there at all.

Either he's a really good actor, Jeremy thought, *or he really is spooked by something in the basement.* Jeremy guessed what was coming next, so he hoped it was the former.

"You two idiots are going to spend the night down there," Mick said, the words coming out in a rush. He seemed to compose himself and resumed his pacing. "You may be thinking that it will be easy, but don't be so sure. The two pledges we had spend the night in the basement last night didn't make it. After a few hours they were begging for us to let them out. It seems they kept getting touched by something. They freaked out."

Jeremy envisioned two young college guys in the dark, working themselves into a state of panic. Of course, the touching was either in their heads or caused by a frat brother who had hidden down there for the express purpose of scaring the pledges. It had to be something like that.

"You're allowed to bring one item down there with you," Mick continued. "Meet me back here in an hour with whatever you want to take with you, and we'll see if either of you can stay the whole night." He looked at them with mock contempt. "I doubt if either one of you will, but we'll see."

"A pillow? That's what you're bringing? A pillow?" Eric chuckled.

The sun was going down as Jeremy headed back to the Delta house. Jeremy shrugged and looked at his best friend questioningly. "I want to be comfortable. Why? What do you think you should bring?"

"I don't think you should bring anything, myself," was Eric's reply, "since I can't imagine why you want to join a fucking fraternity in the first place."

"Hot guys, that's why."

"Yeah, I've seen some of them. They're not all that hot." Eric placed his hands on his hips, accentuating his already feminine walk. "If it were me, I'd bring a knife. That way if any of them fuckers tried to mess with me, I could stab them."

Jeremy laughed. "I don't think I'll be accepted as a Delt if I stab a frat brother."

"Good! Maybe then you'll come to your senses and forget all this frat nonsense. I certainly wouldn't want to join any organization that wanted me to spend the night in some dirty old basement."

Jeremy glanced over at his friend and tried to imagine Eric roughing it on a basement floor. Eric would squeal at the first speck of dirt that got onto his clothing and scream like a girl at any unknown sound. If unseen hands touched him, the boy would probably faint. Even still, Jeremy wished he was spending the night with Eric instead of the rather stuffy Tony.

"I wish you'd change your mind and join with me," Jeremy said. "It would definitely be more fun with you around."

"Honey, they don't let queens like me into fraternities. Maybe I could get into a sorority, though. Teach them girls some clothing and makeup tips."

They had reached the large brick mansion now used as the Delta Tau Delta house. Jeremy hugged his pillow against his chest and sighed. "I guess I'd better get in."

Eric reached out to straighten his friend's collar. "You be good in there. Show them frat boys that we queers aren't afraid of spooks and things that go bump in the night."

"What are you going to do?"

"Me? Honey, I'm headed to the library. Get me some cock. The fourth floor stacks is a great place to go. You can usually find some closet case up there wanting to get his dick sucked. And, provided they don't look like Quasimodo, I'm more than happy to oblige them." Eric wiggled his fingers in farewell and began to walk away.

Jeremy watched him go, feeling a little sad. Much as he hated to admit it, Jeremy thought that Eric was probably right. A small, obviously gay black kid like Eric would never make it into a frat. Not in Indiana, anyway. Guys like Mick would never let up on him, making his life a living hell.

Sighing, Jeremy slowly made his way up the steps to the front door.

Mick, flanked by several other frat brothers, was standing before the basement door. Jeremy and Tony stood in front of them, brandishing their items. Mick eyed Jeremy's pillow with obvious derision. "Into comfort, are we, Pledge?"

Jeremy gave a small shrug. "I thought I'd need something to rest my head on, sir."

Looking at the flashlight in Tony's hands, Mick barked, "And how about you? Afraid of the dark, Pledge?"

"No, sir," Tony barked back. He sounded like some newbie in an army boot camp. "Just thought it might come in handy, sir."

One of Mick's cronies, a husky guy whose name escaped Jeremy, laughed derisively. "Better check his batteries, guys. We wouldn't want them to find themselves in total darkness down there."

Mick's lip curled in amusement. "You've got a point there. Let me see that flashlight, Pledge."

For a moment it looked like Tony was going to protest, but after a short pause he handed the flashlight to Mick. "I just put new batteries in it, sir."

Mick twisted off the end and allowed the batteries to slide out into his hand. "I'm not so sure. These look pretty worn out." He nodded at the overly tall guy next to him. "Ellis, why don't you get the batteries out of the flashlight we keep in the hall? We can replace these with our own. I certainly wouldn't want to send these pledges down there without sufficient light."

While Ellis went to retrieve the other batteries, Jeremy stole a sideways glance over at Tony to see how he was reacting to Mick's obvious sabotage. Tony's face showed no emotion, but he was standing so still that Jeremy suspected he was suppressing some anger. Jeremy didn't blame him. At least Jeremy would have a soft place to rest his head. Tony would be left with a flashlight that would, if it worked at all, give out after only a few minutes.

Once the replacement batteries were fit into place, Mick handed Tony back the flashlight. "I guess that's it, fellas. Any last words?"

"No, sir," Jeremy and Tony answered in unison.

Mick smiled and placed a hand on the doorknob. "Off you go, then. We'll be locking you in, but we'll be here first thing in the morning to let you out. If you get too scared, just pound on the door. I'm not promising anyone will hear, but if we do we'll be sure to let you out." He opened the door dramatically. "If we hear, that is."

Mick and his Delta companions waited only until Jeremy and Tony had made it to the bottom of the stairs before switching off the lights. "Buh-bye!" Mick shouted with mock cheeriness as he slammed and locked the basement door.

Suddenly plunged into pitch blackness, Jeremy felt a momentary dizziness come over him. He reached out and grabbed at where he thought the handrail for the stairs would be. Instead he ended up pawing at Tony's sleeve.

Tony jerked his arm away. "Hey, watch it, dude."

"Sorry. I can't see a damn thing."

A thin, weak beam of light showed as Tony flicked on his flashlight. It didn't illuminate much, but Jeremy welcomed any respite from the complete darkness. At least he could see the wide grin spread across Tony's face. "That's why I brought this. I like to see what I'm dealing with."

Tony played the beam around the room, revealing little other than packing cases and shelf after shelf loaded with sundry tools. Shoved into a corner was a ratty old couch, minus any of its cushions. Any thoughts Jeremy entertained of using it for sleeping on disappeared as he saw several springs poking up through rips in the material.

The Basement

There were cobwebs everywhere. *And where there are cobwebs,* Jeremy thought, *there are spiders.* Jeremy detested spiders.

Sighing, Tony said, "This place is filthy."

"That's putting it mildly," Jeremy agreed. "I don't know about it being haunted, though. No self-respecting ghost would be caught dead down here. Pun intended."

The beam from the flashlight faltered for a moment. Tony gave it a shake and the thin beam brightened a little. "These batteries aren't going to last long," he stated. "Let's find someplace to sit and you can tell me all about this football player that's supposed to still be hanging around. You seem to have all the answers. I've only heard that this place is supposed to be haunted. Can't say I've ever heard the story behind it."

Jeremy followed Tony to an area behind some of the packing cases where they found some broken-down chairs that were serviceable. The wooden chair Tony chose was missing a leg but at least it supported his weight. Jeremy was left with a decrepit wing-back chair that looked like it had been mauled by a tiger. It wasn't the most comfortable of chairs, but it beat sitting on the floor. Once they'd settled, Tony switched off the light to conserve what little power the batteries possessed.

"I don't really know a whole lot about him," Jeremy said, his voice sounding unnaturally loud in the darkness. He adjusted his tone and continued. "Supposedly he was this big football star back in '75 or so. The story goes that after a big game he came back here and hanged himself."

"Did he lose the game or something?"

Jeremy laughed. "No, according to what I heard he always came back here for a clandestine meeting with someone. No one knows who. Anyway, I guess this football player and this girl, whoever she was, always had sex down here in the basement after a win. On this occasion, though, he came here and found a note from her. She'd fallen in love with someone else, so he killed himself."

There was incredulity in Tony's voice. "You mean he hung himself over some chick?"

"Hanged," Jeremy corrected. "He may have been hung, but that's something entirely different. Anyway, yeah, that's the story. Ever since then, people have claimed to see his ghost down here. The Delts usually have pledges spend a night here, and I guess tonight's our turn."

Tony turned on the flashlight and scanned the room. "Well, we seem to be the only ones down here. I guess he's not the most reliable of ghosts."

"It's early yet. He might still make an appearance." Jeremy smiled, realizing that Tony was unable to see his face.

With a bored grunt, Tony switched off the light. "Well, until he shows up, I guess there's not much else to do except get in a little shut-eye."

An image flashed through Jeremy's mind and he could envision Tony, his pants down around his ankles, pumping his hard cock into Jeremy's ass. While a good fuck session would help to pass the time, Jeremy didn't feel comfortable enough with Tony to suggest it, so he replied, "I guess you're right."

Jeremy slouched in his chair and propped his pillow behind his head. After a few minutes he heard Tony's breathing deepen and become more rhythmic. Jeremy envied him. *Getting any sleep,* he thought, *in this sorry excuse for a chair isn't likely.* Nevertheless he closed his eyes, listening to Tony's soft snore.

Jeremy awoke with a start. Momentarily disconcerted, Jeremy realized he'd nodded off after all. As his eyes struggled to make anything out in the blackness, he tried to figure out what had awakened him. It seemed as if someone had tapped him on the arm. He could see nothing, but Jeremy sensed that someone was standing next to his chair. "Tony?" he asked, his voice gruff from sleep.

"Hey," came the reply.

Jeremy sat up straight, listening intently. "Is something happening?" Tony wasn't the skittish type. Jeremy knew that he wouldn't come over to rouse his companion for no reason. Maybe the football player's ghost had decided to make an appearance after all. Jeremy looked around, but the room was pitch black. He wished Tony would switch on his flashlight, if even for just a moment.

"Nothing's happening. Just wanted some company."

Jeremy frowned, wondering what Tony meant by that. He got his answer when a hand grabbed his wrist. Jeremy took a sharp intake of breath as his hand was guided to Tony's crotch. His pledge brother apparently had stripped naked and was standing right next to Jeremy's chair with a very hard—and very large—erection. Jeremy stroked Tony's member, marveling at how good it felt. Tony wasn't exactly his type, but he certainly had a fantastic cock.

"Suck me," Tony said. "Suck that fucking cock."

Jeremy leaned across the arm of the chair and opened his mouth, but before he knew what was happening Tony grabbed him by the hair and forced Jeremy's head forward. Jeremy found his mouth filled with Tony's hot prick. Caught by surprise, Jeremy tried to pull away but found strong hands holding his head in place. Tony began bucking his hips, slamming his dick further and further past Jeremy's lips.

Once the shock of the attack was over, Jeremy relaxed a little. He hadn't thought Tony would be the forceful type, but then he hadn't thought Tony would be the type for man-on-man sex, either. *Tony, you sly dog, you,* Jeremy thought. He managed as much of a smile as he could with Tony's hot cock jammed into his mouth. *I never took you for the rough-and-tumble type, let alone the type to swing both ways.*

Tony emitted a low moan as Jeremy slid an arm up Tony's abdomen to his chest. *Rock hard abs as well. I never would have guessed. I'm going to have to convince this guy to stop wearing those baggy T-shirts. Abs like these should be shown off.*

Jeremy's used his other hand to undo his jeans. His own cock was straining to be free. It wasn't easy to maneuver with Tony holding Jeremy's head tightly in place, but he finally managed to shove his jeans and underwear down far enough to gain access to his own aching member. As he began jacking it, Tony's thrusts increased to a furious pace. He was slamming his cock home so hard that Jeremy knew he was close to coming. He beat his own meat faster, wanting to reach climax as Tony's sweet juice filled his mouth.

Sure enough, in moments Tony let out a guttural growl and his cock exploded in Jeremy's mouth. Jeremy swallowed hard, but the sheer volume of Tony's jizz made it impossible to get all of it. Jeremy's chin became drenched and the thick goo dripped down onto his T-shirt.

Jeremy felt his dick twitch in readiness just as Tony pulled his dick out of his mouth. As he began to shoot, a feeble light came on.

"What the fuck are you doing?" a voice asked.

The light was coming from the three-legged wooden chair, where Tony, sleepy-eyed and fully clothed, was slouching. The weak flashlight didn't illuminate much, but Jeremy could see that much. He quickly looked next to his chair. No one was standing there. *But that can't be,* Jeremy thought, his mind whirling. *If it wasn't Tony feeding me his cock . . .*

"Holy shit," Tony said, running the light up and down Jeremy's body. "You were jacking off. Christ, what a perv."

Jeremy flushed red as he pulled his jeans up. "It's not what you think," he said.

"I think it's exactly what I think," Tony said, snapping off the light. "Try to keep your prick in your pants, will you? I don't want to see that damn thing. Jesus, now I'll have nightmares the rest of the night."

Jeremy felt his chin. The thick come was still there. He hadn't dreamed it. But if it had been real and it hadn't been Tony . . .

Maybe the football player hadn't been meeting a girl. Maybe he had more secrets than anyone suspected . . .

No, it couldn't be . . . could it?

Food Fight Night

Troy Storm

"Yeah, man, the food is finally flying!" The excited fraternity brother next to me let out a yell, deftly dodging a glob of cream pie sailing past. Stripping off his hand-lettered "Food Fight Night" T-shirt—exposing his flabby but pinchable pectorals—the senior brother bellowed another battle howl and charged into the mass of naked male bodies.

Thankfully, this year we had decided to have our traditional initiation rite in the frat house's basement "dungeon," which could be hosed down when the mucky event was over. Last year, we'd decided to have it in the less gloomy upstairs rec room, and we had covered everything with plastic sheeting, including the walls. But thirty horny, naked guys covered in food having sex is not conducive to keeping slippery plastic in place. It took every guy in the frat working for two whole weeks to get the damned place back to where it could be used without us upchucking.

This year we went back to the dungeon but added some fancy disco lights. Nothing like a thick, half-filled slab of chicken dick, perkily bouncing over a packed fistful of freshman gonads, lit up by flashing hot pink spotlights and backlit with eye-rattling streaks of purple and green, to put a brother in a party mood.

The plan of action for Food Fight Night consisted of first herding our naked pledges together and having the rest of our honorable fraternity do stupid things like try to knock a box of condoms off a guy's head by spraying a can of beer at him.

Or finding out which butt cheeks could clutch a greased banana.

Or how much jello a hard dick could scoop out of a tub of the jiggly stuff.

And while our newest members attempted those manly feats of physical skill, the rest of us senior members would pelt them with various vegetables and fruit—preferably overripe—in order to disrupt their concentration.

Though the lowly pledges were ostensibly not permitted to pelt us back, tradition held that some guy should show initiative and sneak in a return zinger, which, of course, none of the pledges would admit to. Whereby the august body of frat brothers, dressed in easily discardable grungy T-shirts and shorts, would call down some untenable punishment on the pledges heads, such as sucking all the seniors' dicks or writing all the seniors' research papers. Whereupon the young bucks would feign outrage and instantly revolt . . . indicating total stupidity on our part, since the new guys now had all the ammunition.

And the foodstuffs would start flying back at us.

There was, of course, nefarious method in our planned madness, since everybody in the fraternity then ends up naked, covered with food, in a pile, grab-assing and wrestling and trying to out-howl and out-curse each other. Eventually, an overly excited hormone kicks in and somebody grabs somebody else's flopping slippery handle in order to bring a man down.

Once a bone is grabbed, we instantly go from food hell to sex hell and the place ends up a total orgy of fucking and sucking until the wee hours.

We have, therefore, fulfilled the educational goal of Food Fight Night, which is getting the fear of sex with another guy out of our pledge's systems—thereby lighting one of the dark corners of a sex-obsessed straight male's mind.

Food Fight Night

The next day, the straight guys will make nervous jokes about what they did—particularly if they had a damned fine time doing it—then soon pretend it never happened and resume their studly places with even more macho verve by humping as many of our fellow sorority sisters as can be talked into letting our hound dogs service their snatches.

There are, however, those of us who wait for the stupid tradition of Food Fight Night with bated balls each year, knowing that the true measure of a man's interest in another man is going to surface in several young bucks, who will need sympathetic understanding and counseling for having discovered . . . and indulged in . . . and been thrilled by . . . their hidden lust.

Possibly several of the nervous group of horny young dudes will need their tottery egos shored up by further exploration of hot, sweaty, man-on-man sexual activity. I am one of the major shorer-uppers.

But that's tomorrow.

Tonight, in the thick of the fight, I let my eyes wander over the juice-drenched pectorals, the chocolate-streaked firm buns, and the jello-anointed dicks, looking for fresh meat.

Richards, a horny sophomore, is the first to grab Anderson, a lean, mean, whipped-cream-covered freshman machine. They go down, clutching each other's butts and balls. A senior wades in and slams one guy's head into the other guy's crotch. Anderson goes down on Richards like a dog on a bone.

Richards's eyes roll back in his head as his jaw drops and Anderson's meat disappears down his throat. A perfect 69.

With a whoop, some other guy grabs his partner's head and shoves it between his legs. Soon, some other guy grabs a butt and starts humping.

I blow the ear-splitting horn and everybody freezes.

I rip open the basket of condoms and start pitching the plastic and tubes of lube. Everybody goes back into action.

"Can I suck you, sir?"

The pledges have to call us 'sir' for the first six weeks. After that, nicknames like Sweet Butt and Deep Tonsils begin to surface.

The request to add his name to my dance card came from Harner, I was pleased to note. The freshman was one of the tastier stud puppies, with a high school gymnastics bod—which meant he would be very flexible—and he sported one of the bigger dicks.

I benevolently placed my hand on the back of his pie-encrusted tangle of dark brunette waves to gently pull him forward. His hot lips suctioned onto my eager, erect manhood like I was the only meat available on a desert island. It always amazes me how competent supposedly straight guys can be at giving head.

As Harner chowed down enthusiastically, over the din and from behind I heard, "Can I fuck your ass, sir? Can I fuck your ass?" in fake, treble, pleading tones.

The smug request came from my old nemesis Benalton. He was a junior who had played with my affections for two solid years on Food Fight Night. Otherwise, he wouldn't give me the time of day. Darkly handsome, each year his muscular frame more eye-gogglingly constructed than the last, he would teasingly wave his weak-knee-inducing meat in my face but always swing it away at the last second.

And I deserved it. During his virginal initiation, when I was a sophomore and he a lowly freshman pledge, I had treated his beautiful butt badly. I hadn't yet then learned how to breach the cherry male hole with respect and care. His obvious discomfort the next couple of weeks—and the sharp rebuke to our fraternity from the Student Health office—brought me low.

Benalton knew I lusted after his hot bod, and the next two

years at Food Fight Night he tormented me—for a few minutes, anyway. Almost instantly, though, some hunky stud's best asset was up my ass or down my gullet and the dark, ever-more-beautiful beauty of Benalton faded from my consciousness. Only to surface the next year—like now.

He was rubbered up and ready and from his massive erection it looked like he had been lifting weights with his dick.

"Don't tease me, man," I yelled over the rising mayhem, feeling an ache in my ass even as I admired the way Harner—the eager young frosh gnawing his way through my crotch—very competently worked another couple of inches of what I had to offer down his gagging throat.

"No shit, dude, I promise to be good," Benalton yelled back, circling around front while reaching over young Harner to tweak my nipples. He leaned his fat-free pile of masculinity teasingly toward me, peering down at the devouring freshman between us before continuing. "The word is you've got one of the tightest love tubes on campus, man. I am butt hungry. I am butt desperate. Mary Lou has been annoyed lately. I'm not getting any."

"Mary Lou is probably pissed because that thing between your leg is outdistancing her sports bra size. How the fuck do you just keep getting bigger?"

"Exactly," he smiled, pleased that I had asked. "By fucking." Damn, he was a killer dude when he showed his beautifully maintained fangs—especially when his gorgeous body was wearing nothing but a coating of creamed spinach and ketchup. "The more I work it, the bigger it gets." A dark eyebrow crooked up as he moved closer to stretch out a muscular arm to reach around and stroke his big, probing fingers up and down my crack. "You still owe me one, remember? A big one. You bad-assed my butt, dude. You gotta pay."

Damn, the man was hot, and, damn, the hot mouth of the eager young stud at my crotch was twisting my testes. My butthole quivered in excited anticipation and fearful dread.

A hunky straight man, horse hung, paying my gay ass back for having buggered him in the heat of Food Fight Night years ago. Benalton had waited and planned and now he was ready to strike deep into my quivering hole while his food-covered iron was hot. Sounded cool.

If only my anxious anus could take it.

I accepted my fate . . . and nodded.

The muscular dude moved back around behind me. I bent over Harner and playfully paddled his butt, mooning my hot nemesis. Over the groans and gasps and plaintive cries surrounding us, I thought I heard an appreciative grunt, which was probably more my hoping Benalton recognized prime pucker when it was stuck in his face than him actually being that impressed. More'n likely he had already had every type of hole imaginable on campus presented for his drilling.

He put his hands on my hips and tightened his grip. At my crotch, Harner sucked like a starving calf. Suddenly, mama cow butted her way into my rear end hoping to rescue her baby boy.

Cow! Hell, no, it was the whole damn herd that had stampeded up my rectum. I opened my mouth to scream—stunned at how Benalton had grown so hard and so huge—but somebody slammed an overripe peach in my face. I hacked out the mushy muck, my spasming sphincter fighting the huge pole of manhood blasting up my insides.

"Right on, men!" One of our football types charged by with a totally blessed-out blond kid thrown over his wide-receiver shoulders. The footballer smacked his captive's smooth, pink ass and clutched at his tight nutsack. "I got me some dessert!" the big stud yelled cheerfully as the succulent pledge beamed.

Food Fight Night

Benalton's powerful front molded itself to my rigid back. His hips began a hard pistoning. His giant dong slammed deep into my awed anus and ripped back out. Before my gasping butthole could collapse shut, he drove his stake back into my innards, aiming for my heart.

His pinching fingers tore at my nipples. "Oh, man, your ass is beautiful," he murmured, gnawing on my ear, as he continued to batter his leg of beef into my agonized anal alleyway. "At first, I just wanted to rip you open like you had me, but then Student Health got on the frat's tail and you started the Don't Be An Abused Butt classes and saved a lot of other tender holes from getting hurt. I thought that was cool, dude."

My butthole was numb, my colon had shut down, and my insides were creamed meat.

"I figured," he grunted, "we both were too young (Bam! Bam! Bam! His piledriver drove into me.) and too fucking inexperienced to know how to do it right. (Bam! Bam! Bam!) And you did apologize. Or tried to. Sorry about that, man. I just wasn't ready to give you the time of day."

He paused momentarily from pummeling my ass and took a deep breath. So did my hole.

"The word around the frat is that you like 'em big and hard. And I had seen the look in your eyes when I shoved my dick in your face on Food Fight Night. So after Mary Lou went into lockdown, I figured it was payback time and maybe time to accept your apology. (Bam! Bammity bam!) I'm plenty big and I'm plenty hard. You like it? Has it been worth waiting for, man? (Bam! De bam!) 'Cause it sure as hell feels phenomenal from back here."

It was . . . unbelievable . . . great . . . fantastic. Sensation seeped back into my stunned nerve endings, starting lava boiling deep in the butt volcano he was ramming solid liquid fire into.

Harner was getting dizzy from being smacked around by the furious slamming of Benalton's hips. The frosh pledge pulled off my dick, shook his head and began to beat me off. Immediately beefy brother Panglos threw a muscular, hairy leg between the two of us and stepped in to shove his fruit-drenched meat between Harner's surprised chops. Twisting around, the interloper kissed me on the mouth—in order to lick off the chocolate sauce, most likely—and rubbered me up, as Harner sucked him and Benalton continued to rip open my now-very-accommodating backside.

Panglos guided my rock-hard dick into his hole and backed up against me, his cuddly buns snuggling against my pubes.

"Your ass is the best," Benalton yelled at the top of his lungs from behind me. "You know that, dudes?" He bellowed to the nonlistening, otherwise occupied throng. "I've fucked all the fuckable butts in this school, but this brother's ass is the fucking *best.*"

I dropped my head back rapturously, he leaned in and clamped his open mouth to mine. Slamming his dick up my ass so hard it seemed to thrust against my tonsils, combined with the way he swabbed my uvula with his tongue, it felt like Benalton was soon gonna be lapping the end of his own meat.

The thought of my insides being so thoroughly reamed tickled me. I shot a load up Panglos' butt. He let loose with one of the university football yells that was echoed throughout the room by his fellow fucking frat dudes. From the way his body tensed and jerked I figured he was emptying a gutful into Harner.

Benalton's massive musculature, wrapped around my body, gripped me with a boa constrictor clutch. Lightning bolts shot from my abused tits throughout my body to singe the flattened hairs around my hole.

Inside, Benalton's dick lurched ever larger, then, cobralike, struck my innards with white-hot bolts of cream. His big body quivered and shook. More and more manmilk blobbed against the bulging rubber tube wrapping his dick and ballooning inside my ass.

I had to admit, I had just received the epitome of buttfucks. Benalton and I were buds again.

For the rest of the evening, we stuck to each other, in as many different configurations as our holes and poles could figure out.

Eventually—especially with the new frat members—asses began to rebel and dicks refused to bone up. The guys staggered and crawled off into the far corner of the room, where a hose had been attached, to wash off their come-encrusted vegetable and fruit coating.

Which led to the water fight—the last section of the ritual.

Benalton and I stayed bolted together in a 69 as the guys hosed us off. Soon, still screwing ourselves blind, we were the only two sex hounds left in the room.

The dark beauty rolled onto his back, stretching and yawning like the bronzed young lion he was. I crawled up to straddle him, sinking my ass over his once-again massive erection, my now-happy hole easily and fervently ingesting the huge protein pole.

"I was a shit," I said. "You were so hot. And you never complained while I was busting your butt." Suddenly I realized with some pride, I also had not let on how badly his initial retaliatory fuck that evening had chopped my nuts. I stroked my hands up and down his front as he smugly watched, gripping my bone and jerking me off in a matching rhythm.

He snagged a forlorn pitted cherry swimming alongside us and propped it between his full lips. "Eat me," he grinned.

My tongue followed the cherry down his throat.

The Headmaster

Zavo

It was my first semester as a pre-law student at a prestigious college in upstate New York. After high school graduation I had had no solid plans to continue my education, but my father certainly had. And those plans resulted in my being at this college. His old alma mater. I was sharing a room with Randall Simms, who was also a freshman. It was the fourth week of classes, and I was comfortably settled in my new routine. Randall and I were both pledging the most popular fraternity at the school. We had subsequently learned that both our dads had been members of the same fraternity. I had immediately developed a crush on Randall, and my feelings had continued to deepen as the semester unfolded. But he had never reciprocated any feelings for me; he was hot and heavy with someone from his hometown. His name was Chris Durham, and I had met him several times because he visited every other weekend. I had immediately disliked him, and not just because of my crush on Randall or my deepening feelings. I didn't trust him, and I didn't like the way he treated Randall.

But Chris's visits had suddenly stopped, with no explanation from Randall. Nor did I ask for one. We had become instant friends, but I was pretty sure that's all we would ever be. It was a Friday, and I didn't have a class till ten. Randall was in the shower, and I was in my favorite overstuffed rocking chair, a gift from my mother, reading a book for my American literature class. However, I was having trouble concentrating because my mind kept returning to the latest hazing prank we had been involved in, which had taken place the previous night. We were several weeks into our pledge, and the events continued to be more and more bizarre and reckless. The night before had been not merely reckless, but downright illegal. The whole group of us, twenty pledges plus twenty of our fraternity brothers, had broken into our archrival's fraternity house. We had been armed with paint, eggs, and tomatoes. It was in retaliation for the beating of one of our pledges a few days before. While rivalries between fraternity houses were most often good-natured, this had been going on for more than two decades, and it was continuing to get more and more violent and ugly.

My train of thought was interrupted when Randall suddenly burst into the room. He was six months older than I was. He stood well over six feet, with light blond hair and skin the color of porcelain. We always joked that if he were to spend any time in the sun he would burst into flames. He had a towel wrapped around his bottom half. I could see the large cockhead underneath the cotton material. He moved to his dresser, unwrapped the towel, and began drying himself. My eyes instantly went to his crotch. His cock was long and thick, with a nicely shaped head. His pubic hair was reddish blond and thick. The same reddish blond hair covered his muscular chest and stomach, as well as his arms and legs. His nipples were pink and slightly puffed. I imagined them between my teeth. It was then that Randall noticed I was staring at him. He smiled, and assumed a bashful pose, with the towel half hiding his crotch.

"Don't check me out, Bryan."

I responded with a feeble "I wasn't," to which he just laughed.

"Actually, I don't mind if you look."

I stared at him for a moment, then placed my book on the floor.

"Okay. Come over here so I can get a better look."

He dropped the towel on the floor and came around the end of the bunk beds and stood before me. His dick was already hardening; even half hard it was already long and fat. Without hesitation I grabbed it and began stroking it with a thumb and forefinger. He moaned softly and stepped closer, till his knees were pressed against the chair. His dick was fully hard now, and a good nine inches. His balls matched the rest of his equipment, rolling around in their sack of silky flesh. The left one was slightly larger and hung a little lower than the right.

"Suck on it," he said huskily.

I leaned forward and took the head into my mouth, swirling my tongue around it and nipping it gently with my teeth. After a few more swirls of my tongue, I swallowed the head and as much of the thick shaft as I could. It tasted slightly of the soap from his recent shower. I surprised myself when I found my nose buried deep in his crotch hair. In addition to the soap, his individual scent, one that I had become so enamored of, now filled my nostrils. I began bobbing up and down on his shaft, while he pumped his hips in rhythm with my head. After several minutes of this he abruptly pulled his pole out of my mouth.

"This is nice," he murmured. "But I'm going to be late for class, so let me drive. You sit still and hold out your tongue."

I scooted forward on the chair and stuck out my tongue as requested. Randall placed his hand on the back of my head and laid his cock atop my tongue. It was warm and heavy resting there. He then began sliding his prick back and forth, and the sensation was incredible. As my hands were free, I used one to knead his ball sack, while with the other I probed between the cheeks of his ass with my index finger, searching for his hole. When I made contact I began strumming it, and he moaned his appreciation. He was sliding his stiffer faster and faster on my tongue, and it was getting hard to hold it in place. Rivulets of sweat were running down Randall's torso, pooling in his crotch hair. As my finger slid inside his hole, I felt his balls roll up snug to the base of his shaft. I prepared myself for the imminent eruption.

"I'm gonna come!" he cried.

I felt the first blob of his spooge land on my tongue, followed by more and more of the sticky stuff. If I looked cross-eyed I could see the substantial pile he was building. When he was spent, he stepped back from the chair, and I slid my tongue back in my mouth, swallowing the entire load.

"That was great head, Bryan. But I really have to run. I'll be back later this afternoon, and we can further explore you and your talents."

"I'll be here, Randall."

He bent down and kissed me, his tongue pushing past my lips. He paused a moment and stared into my eyes, seemingly wanting to say something. But he just smiled, dressed hurriedly, and left for class.

I was off to my first morning class, and it was my favorite: history, with Professor Douglas. As I walked my thoughts again turned to the events of the night before. While inside the rival frat house I had been caught by one of its members. I was taken by surprise, because we had believed the house was virtually empty while the brothers were off at one of their hazing events. The guy had torn off my mask and recognized me because he was in my archery class. He had my arms pinned behind my back when Randall came up behind him and knocked him out with one punch. If he hadn't, I'd probably be in jail right now. But I had no doubt there was going to be some kind of dire repercussion. I quickly took my seat in class and immediately lost track of the events that had led up to the Spanish-American war. Suddenly there was a knock on the classroom door and the dean's secretary, Miss Pilkington, entered. All eyes turned to watch her, as she was known as a real hard case across campus. Without a word she handed the professor a note, then turned and left. He read the note, looked directly at me, then folded it and put it in his pocket. A sinking feeling began in the pit of my stomach. When the lecture was over and I got up to leave, Professor Douglas called me to his desk.

"Bryan, Dean Matthews wishes to see you in his office as soon as you can."

The feeling of dread deepened when I heard this.

"Thanks, Professor Douglas. I have an hour before my next class so I'll head there now. Did he say what it was about?"

"No, Bryan, but he is the Dean, so I'm sure he doesn't simply want to chat about the weather."

With that withering statement adding to the weight I already felt on my shoulders, I went down the hall and out the front door. I paused on the steps to control my runaway breathing. Dean Matthews's office was located in the center of the campus. We had all been made aware of this during orientation, and it was only a short walk from here. The sunshine of a fall day did nothing to dispel my deepening unease. When I reached the administration building I quickly found his office. I opened a large wooden door and found myself in a small room as silent as a tomb. It contained an enormous wooden desk, with the stern secretary perched behind it, and several rather uncomfortable-looking chairs. That was the extent of the furnishings. Miss Pilkington eyed me as if she'd rather skin me than allow me into her sacred area. She obviously knew who I was, because she didn't ask my name. Without speaking to me she got up and knocked softly on a large wooden door to her left. I didn't hear a response, but she opened it, poked her head in, then came back and sat at her desk.

"The Dean will see you now."

When I stood, my legs felt like rubber, but I managed to stay upright as I opened the door and stepped inside the Dean's office. It was large, in keeping with the importance of the man who oversaw the entire college, and who also still taught one or two classes. The walls were paneled in a dark wood, with two windows facing the courtyard below. The wall he shared with Miss Pilkington had wainscoting of the same dark wood for the first three feet, then glass windows to the ceiling. However, you couldn't see through it into Miss Pilkington's office. The dean was sitting behind a desk that took up an entire wall. Two chairs faced it. The wall directly behind him was covered in framed diplomas, maps, aerial pictures of the school, and numerous sports memorabilia. An American flag stood in the corner to my right. The rest of the walls that weren't windows were taken up by bookshelves, with what looked hundreds of books stuffed onto them. The desk he was sitting behind was covered with papers, books, and magazines. The only clear space was a large blotter.

Dean Matthews was quite an imposing figure, one that I had never been this close to before. He stood to greet me as I approached his desk.

"Mr. Mason, please have a seat. How are you on this fine morning?"

I opened my mouth to speak but nothing came out. I quickly cleared my throat and responded with a weak "Fine."

He was several inches above six feet, with broad shoulders and a thick torso. I think it was safe to say he had played sports when he was in college. He was wearing light brown corduroy pants that hugged the muscles in his legs, as well as his crotch. The head of his cock was plainly visible to the left of his zipper, and it was good sized. He had a white dress shirt on with a dark brown tie. Beneath it I could see the V of his undershirt. His pectorals were nicely outlined beneath the cotton material. He had a mop of light brown hair sprinkled with gray, and a large mustache and sideburns to match. A faint cologne wafted across the desk. As I stood there I could feel him taking the measure of me with his eyes. I had not been prepared for how handsome and dashing he was.

He went to one of the windows and stared out it, not saying a word for several minutes. Suddenly, he turned to me, an inscrutable expression on his face.

"I understand you are a freshman, Bryan. And I further understand you're pledging the most popular fraternity at this college. In fact, it's the same one I pledged when I was here, and your father as well."

I couldn't hide my surprise at the mention of my father. I knew he had been in the fraternity here, and I had heard numerous ribald stories of his initial hazing, and the years after he had been accepted. But I had never heard him speak of Headmaster Matthews.

"And as I look at you, Bryan, I see a striking resemblance to your father. He and I were good friends when we attended here. Very good friends. It's out of respect for him that I am doing this. Being the most popular fraternity does not excuse what you and your brothers did last night. Destruction of property is a serious offense. Fortunately for you, I was able to persuade the school board that I would handle this matter, ensuring it didn't repeat itself and that the guilty parties were disciplined. And from the report I got this morning, you were the only one that was identified. That is why I called you to my office today. As such, you will be responsible for the cleanup and restoration of the damages. But, right now there is something else I need you to do."

He turned from the window and came around to stand beside me. His cock was level with my face, and I couldn't miss the growing lump it made under the corduroy. He looked down at me, and I in turn stared up at him. The lust in his eyes was unmistakable. This close his sheer size was even more overpowering. He grabbed a ruler that was lying on his desk. I was starting to get a weird feeling about this meeting.

"I believe in old-fashioned punishment, Bryan. Please hold out your left hand, palm up."

When I did he grabbed it and, without warning, whacked it with the ruler. I yelped in surprise, but as I started to pull my hand away from him he grabbed it and, placing it on the lump at his crotch, began rubbing it vigorously.

"This will take away most of the sting."

After a few strokes of my hand the lump swelled considerably. He then pushed my hand away gently, unzipped his pants, and slid them and a pair of white boxers down to his knees. His dick was long and thick, the fat crown already leaking its pre-juice. The smell of his crotch filled my nostrils, intoxicating me.

"I think we can help each other out in this situation, Bryan. Would you agree? I'm sure your parents, especially your father, would not want you kicked out of this college for the foolish, stupid prank you and your fraternity brothers perpetrated. I don't think he expected a response, and I obliged him.

"Lick it," he said softy, his voice husky with lust.

I was not going to deny him. I lapped up his juice, then grabbed his ball sack and pulled it to my mouth. The large twin orbs swayed in their heavy sack of flesh. I pulled at the few hairs that speckled the skin. I spit into my hand and spread the fluid the length of his cock, then grabbed it in my right hand. It was thick and heavy. I then took the flared head into my mouth, relishing its silky softness. I swirled my tongue over it before sinking down as much of the shaft as I could. When I opened my eyes I was staring into his thick patch of dark brown crotch hair. I continued to hold his cock deep down my throat, while sucking on it softly. He placed his hand on the back of my head and murmured words of encouragement. I then sawed back to the fat knob, swirled my tongue once more over it, then began bobbing up and down on his stiffer. After several minutes he pulled his dick from me. I reached for it but he held me back.

"I don't want to come just yet, Bryan. Now, stand up, turn around, and face my desk." I did as he'd commanded, pretty sure of what was about to happen and wanting it very much. He stepped behind me and began stroking the front of my pants; I was already hard and ready to go. He unzipped them and pulled them down to my ankles, closely followed by my boxers. He spread my thighs apart and bent me forward over the desk. He began running his finger along the crack of my ass. It tickled, and I wiggled my ass, enticing him to explore further. Imagine my surprise when he paused and the next thing I felt was the smack of the ruler against my right cheek. It smarted tremendously, and I bit my lip to keep from crying out. Another stroke followed on the same cheek, then he moved to the other one. The same number of hits landed there. There was a slight pause, and Dean Matthews began to rub the right cheek vigorously, again taking some of the sting of the ruler away. He did the same with the left. When he was done there, I received two more whacks on each cheek with the instrument, followed by his soothing palms. When I looked down I realized I had made a sizable puddle of jism on his blotter. You could have hung a coat on my dick it was so hard; obviously my body was highly aroused by the spanking I was receiving.

After a good ten minutes of this, he suddenly stopped. He spread the cheeks of my ass and I jumped when I felt his tongue swirling between them. He licked all along the crack, avoiding my sweet spot, before finally driving his tongue deep into my chute.

"Lick that hole, professor."

My words spurred him to greater efforts, and he began lapping at my hole as if it were his salvation. His tongue was suddenly replaced by a finger, which began poking at my tender opening. I heard him spit, and I gasped as the large digit ceased its probing and slid deep inside me with no warning. He began plunging it in and out, and I moved my ass in time with his thrusts. After a few more lunges he suddenly withdrew it.

"I have something I think is much more your size, Bryan."

He reached over my shoulder and pulled a silver tube from underneath a pile of papers. I heard the cap flip open, and then a cool gel was slathered on my asshole, and then inside me as well by a very thorough finger. When Dean Matthews was satisfied I was well greased, he withdrew his finger and replaced it with the head of his cock. He held it there for a minute, rubbing the large knob over my brown hole. I wiggled my ass back against it, wanting him—no, needing him—inside of me. And he didn't deny me any longer. With one giant push the head popped through and he penetrated me steadily till his prick was completely in me. I felt the mysterious muscle deep inside my ass swell when the fat crown struck it. His crotch hair tickled the cheeks of my ass. He held his dick deep inside me, making me feel every inch of it, then withdrew till only the head remained inside. He then sank into me once again, held it still, then began thrusting in and out of me steadily, his stiffer going deep each time. I was sprawled across the desk, gripping the other side of it to keep from being propelled over it. Papers and magazines were falling onto the floor. I was sure Miss Pilkington wondered what the hell was going on in here.

"God, Bryan, I'm gonna come!"

His shout had to have been heard in the outside office and several feet down the hall. And I was right behind him. As he pinned me to the desk and flooded my asshole with his jiz, I sprayed a puddle all over his blotter. When he was spent he planted several kisses on my back, then pulled his cock out of me; it made a loud sucking noise. I stood up, tugged up my pants and boxers and turned around to face him. He pulled me to him and kissed me deeply, his tongue sliding between my lips and exploring my mouth. He then held my head and stared into my eyes, a smile playing about his lips.

"I think you've learned your lesson, Bryan."

"I'm not so sure, Dean," I whispered. "Perhaps I need to come back for more schooling."

He laughed and kissed me again.

"I think that can be arranged."

I lay on my bed, thinking about what had happened with Dean Matthews earlier this morning. The smell of his crotch lingered on my fingers, while the taste of his cock was still heavy in mouth. I began rubbing my crotch, remembering his dick in my mouth, and the ruler and his hands on my ass. I undid my pants and slid them and my boxers down to my knees. I had just spit into my hand and given the old stiffer a few welcome strokes, when I heard a key in the lock, the door opened, and Randall came bursting in. When he saw me lying on the bed, he quickly shut the door behind him. A big smile lit up his face.

"You're not gonna start without me, are you?"

"I was just getting warmed up," I replied.

The smile on his lips was mirrored in his eyes as he began undressing slowly, tantalizingly. As always, the sight of his muscular, hairy torso turned me on. As he pulled down his jeans and boxers his hard pole slapped up against his stomach, depositing a small smear of his early juice. He stepped out of both garments and lay next to me. I turned to face him, and began playfully rubbing my cock against his. He leaned over and kissed me full on the lips deeply and for several minutes. I grabbed his dick and began squeezing it, while he did the same to mine. All the while we simply stared into each other's eyes, not saying a word. He leaned in and kissed me again, then stood up and lay back down with his head at my feet. He then flipped onto his hands and knees and straddled me. His cock was now poised above my mouth, with his mouth directly over my own stiffer. I placed my hands on his hips and began licking the head of his dick. He moaned loudly and tried to push his pole immediately into my mouth. But I held his hips firmly for a few more licks before allowing him to slide in completely, which caused his ball sack to rest on the bridge of my nose. He meanwhile was steadily sawing up and down on my pole, while probing my asshole with several fingers. On his next upward swipe he released my cock, inched down a little, and began licking my hole. With his prick deep down my throat and his tongue probing my spot, my eruption came quickly, surprising me. As Randall slipped two fingers inside me I shot my load in the hollow of his throat. When I was spent, he scooped up my come and ate it, then took the reins and began pistoning his cock in and out of my mouth. I wet my index finger and without any warning slid it deep inside him. He cried out and I felt his warm fluid shooting down my throat. I swallowed it all, and licked his pole clean when he was done. He swung around till he was facing me, kissed me on the lips, then got up and began dressing.

"You're the best friend a guy could ever have, Bryan. I have to go to the library and do some research for my Economics term paper. I'll meet you back here around six and we can go to dinner."

"Sounds good. See you later, friend."

For the next several weeks, Randall and I became acquainted with every inch of each other's bodies. Chris made no more weekend visits, and no mention of him was ever made. I continued to receive regular discipline from Headmaster Matthews. And my retelling of these episodes always proved tremendously arousing for Randall. He was not jealous at all.

It was Friday, and tonight was the last night of hazing. After tonight we would learn which of the pledges had made the cut. Of the twenty original pledges, we were now left with ten. Randall and I left our dorm room in the late afternoon for the fifteen-minute walk to the frat house. It was off campus, as all fraternity houses were required to be. When Randall and I had begun pledging, I was immediately glad that I was going through it with someone I knew. It had made all the hazing that much more tolerable. We had never known at what hour of the day or night we were going to be called to the main house. But when we had been summoned, we had gone immediately.

"Are you worried about what's going to happen tonight, Bryan?"

"A little. But as long as you're here, I think I'll be just fine."

He squeezed my hand and smiled. "That's exactly how I feel."

When we reached the house Randall went up the steps and knocked on the front door. It was answered immediately by the president himself.

"Welcome, lowly pledges. Please come in."

As we stepped into the wide hall we were grabbed from behind and blindfolded. We were then marched down a long hall and several flights of stairs. I wondered if we were in the fabled basement. Neither one of us had as yet been in this room. It was the holy of holies for the fraternity, and only official brothers were allowed to see and use it on a regular basis. After going down another short hallway, I heard a door open, and then we came to a stop. Wherever we were, there was no discernible noise.

"Take your clothes off" were the first words spoken. But the speaker did not identify himself.

I quickly undressed, immediately aware of a slight chill in the air. When I was completely naked, I was startled when my hands were pulled roughly behind my back and bound with a soft material. As soon as this was done a hand grabbed my stiffer and began stroking it, while another hand began caressing my ball sack.

"Nice" was murmured by someone unknown, although the voice sounded familiar. Of course this fondling caused me to become fully hard, which elicited a soft whistle from whoever was holding my cock.

Without further ado I was walked backward till my legs hit the edge of something soft and I fell backward onto what I took to be a large sofa. At the same time I realized there was someone sitting on either side of me. I could feel warm, hairy flesh touching my legs, and the smells of their sweat and cologne also permeated my nostrils. But I didn't recognize Randall as being one of them. Without warning a hand again grabbed my pole and began stroking it softy. It was quickly replaced by a warm tongue that swirled over my cockhead, pausing several times to tentatively probe my piss slit. The tongue was then gone, and a pair of lips took its place. They slowly engulfed the fat knob, then sank down the length of my cock till they were nestled in my crotch hair. They paused before slowly spiraling back to the large crown. They sucked it briefly once more, then began sawing slowly up and down, using just the right amount of suction to draw my ass up from the sofa each time. I was moaning softly, and small whimpers of pleasure were escaping from me nonstop. These mixed with the moans and other noises of pleasure from the guys sitting beside me. I lay back against the sofa and simply gave in to the wonderful suction on my stiffer. Before too much longer I began to feel the telltale signs of my impending explosion. But the guy to my left was to beat me, for the air was filled with loud cries of "I'm coming, I'm coming." As I began to spew my own juice into an eagerly awaiting mouth, it was greedily swallowed without hesitation. When I was spent I was licked clean.

Without warning, the blindfold was removed, and I was pulled roughly to my feet. As my eyes grew accustomed to the gloom, it appeared that we were indeed in the basement, but I had no way to confirm this. To my left were my fellow pledges, all naked as I was. Randall was next to me. I was on the end. Behind us, against the wall, was a row of couches. And standing directly in front of me was what I at first took to be my eyes playing tricks on me. It was a man, but he was garbed as no man I had ever seen before. He was tall and solidly built and, while muscular, not overly so. He was more on the beefy side. He was wearing black leather boots that rose to his knees. Above each boot was several inches of hairy, well-muscled leg, suddenly broken by a black loincloth. His chest was bare but hairy and muscled as well. This incredible ensemble was topped off by a black leather hood with holes for the eyes and mouth, and breathing slits at the nostrils. Standing behind this man were our fraternity brothers. They were all naked, cocks at full attention.

It was then that I saw the raised plywood dais to my far left, several feet past the line of pledges. On top of it was what appeared to be a mattress, covered in a black sheet. I had no time to wonder what it was for, though, as the masked man in front of me began speaking.

"Pledges, I am the master of this fraternity, and I have been for many, many years. And I have a surprise for all of you. For weeks now you've been told that tonight is the final event to determine who shall be made honorary fraternity brothers. However, I'm here to tell you that you ten here tonight will all be inducted into the fraternity. The servicing you each just received is the first part of your official welcome. Now, let's begin part two so the drinking and celebrating can begin."

As if on cue, the brothers turned and filed toward the dais till they were in a line parallel to and facing it. When they were assembled the master continued.

"Each one of you will be called to come to the mattress and position yourselves on your hands and knees. By doing this, you will be offering yourselves to your brothers and me. But, before we begin, I will reveal myself unto you, which is the greatest secret we all share."

The man pulled his mask over his head to reveal he was Dean Matthews. As I looked at the lustful faces of my fellow pledges, I had the sudden realization that I was not the only one to receive punishment in his office.

"Okay, pledges, let's begin."

When the first pledge was called, he crawled onto the mattress then rose on his hands and knees. Dean Matthews knelt behind him, and the pledge offered up his sweet bum. The dean entered him swiftly, with that big cock I knew so well, and proceeded to plow his ass while the rest of us watched, breathless. But after only a few minutes, he suddenly withdrew. He crawled off the mattress, only to be immediately replaced by the next brother in line. Thus it went till all of the brothers had sampled the new pledge. He was then dismissed and the next pledge was called. When it was Randall's turn I watched, mesmerized, as he was put through his paces. I was amazed that none of our brothers had yet to blow a load inside one of the new pledges. When it was my turn, Professor Matthews greased me up and, before entering me, whispered "Hello, old friend."

His thrusts were deep and powerful, as they had been each time we met in his office for my punishment. But all too soon he was withdrawing, and a new prick took his place. When the last brother was done penetrating me, they reformed their line, with the headmaster in the middle, and began stroking their cocks while we watched. The dean was the first to blow, his spunk slopping onto the mattress. The rest followed in quick succession. When they were all spent, a curtain was drawn aside revealing a table which held champagne, wine, beer, pizzas, and hoagies. Dean Matthews handed a glass of champagne to everyone and raised his own glass.

"To the new pledges! May they bring new and long life to the fraternity!"

This was met with a hearty cheer from all, and as alcohol continued to flow, the rest of the night gave way to many more sexual encounters.

Randall and I got home when the sun was just peeking over the horizon. We were both completely worn out, and smelled of champagne, beer, and come. We quickly showered and, as I lay on my bed, I was surprised when Randall lay next to me, his warm skin feeling nice against mine. He began rubbing his dick up and down the crack of my ass, then simply lodged it there and wrapped his arms around me.

"I love you, Bryan."

I was taken aback by his abrupt confession, but had known for several weeks how I felt about him.

"I love you too, Randall. And I have to finally ask what happened with Chris. And, are you on the rebound?"

"No. Chris and I broke up. We had been having problems for a long time. However, it was exacerbated when I realized I had feelings for you. And that happened almost from our first meeting. As my feelings for you grew, it became obvious I needed to leave Chris."

I smiled up at him and he squeezed me tighter as we drifted off to sleep.

Calculus and Condoms

Anne Cain

"I'm sick of this shit!" Gage tossed his backpack on to the floor and gave it a kick for good measure.

The bag skidded across the linoleum to rest at Nathan's feet. The zipper across the top was broken, and some of the textbooks spilled out into jumbled pile. Nathan reached over, his beat-up desk chair creaking under the shift in weight. He picked up the ugly, puke-green textbook with a jumble of equations printed across the cover.

"Calculus, again?" Nathan asked, one eyebrow cocked at his roommate.

"Fuck!" Gage collapsed on the lower bunk against the far wall. Nathan's bed.

"I take that as a yes," Nathan croaked. His mouth had gone completely dry. He watched Gage stretch out width-wise across the messy sheets, his long, beautiful body barely fitting on the narrow mattress. Gage clutched the pillow to his face to smother another cry of frustration.

Shit, the blankets and the pillowcases were going to be covered in Gage's smell—that delicious mixture of body spray, sweat, and sunshine. Gage spent a lot of time studying on the grass under the banyan trees in the courtyard outside the dorms; he liked being outdoors, and the span of golden tan, toned skin that peeked out from the bottom hem of his shirt attested to his love for the California sun—while the swelling erection between Nathan's thighs attested to his love for that sun-kissed flesh.

He could jack off right now on the sight of Gage lying helpless like that, legs spread wide open as they dangled over the edge of the bed. The man's baggy jeans did abso-fucking-lutely *nothing* to hide the mound of cock and balls at his crotch. A shadow under the fly traced the contour of a fat, pointed tip, the head of his dick, and not for the first time Nathan suspected the guy was circumcised. He'd like to find out for sure, though, using a thorough examination with hands and lips. Hell, yeah.

Nathan squirmed while he rubbed his palm over the front of his sweats, his erection kicking against each stroke. The damn chair creaked under his shifting weight again, and Gage tossed the pillow aside with a flustered sigh. Nathan jerked his hand away from his boner and swiveled around to face the desk again, his heart pounding. Gage had no clue how badly he worked up Nathan's sex drive, torturing him with glimpses of his penis whenever he dressed for classes in the morning or when they bumped into each other in the dorm showers.

"I don't know what the hell I'm going to do," Gage moaned.

Do me, Nathan begged silently. *You can shove that monster of a cock up my ass or in my throat all night long.*

"That professor hates my guts," Gage continued, oblivious to Nathan's queer, dirty fantasies involving his cock and box after box of Trojans.

"I can't imagine anyone hating your guts," Nathan sighed. The pillow smacked him on the back of his head.

"Trust me, this prick does," Gage growled. "He has it in for the entire class, as a matter of fact. Only one person out of twenty-two is getting a B. The rest of us are struggling to hold onto our Cs."

Nathan tried not to think about the part of Gage he struggled *not* to hold on to. Using the pillow to cover his erection, he swiveled back around. The situation did sound pretty grave. Gage was a serious student, a year ahead of Nathan. Sure, he partied every once in a while—what college junior didn't?—but he worked hard for his grades, too. He hardly went on dates and had never brought a girl up to the dorms; he was usually too busy cramming to fit sex into his schedule. And being the selfish dick that he was, Nathan was happy over the lack of girlfriends. It helped fuel his hopeless dream that he might ride the sexy piece of meat sleeping in the bunk on top of him one night.

Nathan eyed his friend now, noticing the dark circles under Gage's eyes, the frustration tensing the muscles in his neck and shoulders. He looked stressed and worried. Probably could've used a good fuck right now to relax. Nathan almost offered, but chickened out a split second before blurting out the proposition. He sighed. "This instructor is really giving you trouble, isn't he?"

"I need to pass this class to make it into the engineering program," Gage rubbed his eyes with the heel of his palms. "If he flunks me on the midterms with some trick question, I'm screwed."

Oh, God . . . I'd love to be screwed by you, Gage. Nathan clutched that pillow so hard, he thought he'd squeeze the stuffing out. But all mindless, animal lusting aside, Gage was his friend and in need of help.

"I have an idea." Nathan licked his lips. "But if things go wrong . . . it could be bad."

"How bad?"

"We'd most likely get kicked out," Nathan admitted. "Cheating really rubs the administration the wrong way."

"Forget it," Gage sat up, brushing some of his long, dark bangs out of his eyes. "I'll drop out of the class and try taking it again next semester."

"That'll set you back half a year," Nathan argued.

"Better that than risk you getting fucked up, too." Gage leaned forward on his elbows, dark brows scrunched over honey brown eyes filled with concern.

Nathan could've jumped him right there. Pushed Gage back on to the bed, kissed that sweet mouth and ridden his cock until the sun came in through the dorm room window. He swallowed, clearing his throat from the edge of lust and affection that threatened to spill out.

"You've heard that saying, right? 'Friends help you move; real friends help you move bodies'?" Nathan stood up, confident enough in his control over his own body to keep another stiffy from tenting the front of his sweat pants.

"What are you planning?" Gage's eyes went wide.

Nathan touched his shoulder. "We're going to sneak into that guy's office and find the answer sheet for the midterm."

They moved through the dark, empty hall, straining to catch any sound that campus security was around, or that a professor had stayed to work late in his or her office. The silence encouraged them to keep moving, and Nathan led the way towards the Math & Sciences wing. Gage caught the back of his shirt.

"This is it." He pointed to the door at his left. "Now what?"

"Give me your ID," Nathan whispered, hand outstretched.

Gage obediently fished his wallet out from the back pocket of his jeans and withdrew the plastic card. Nathan noticed a slim condom package also wedged in the same slot. He must've been staring with a strange expression on his face because when he looked up, Gage's cheeks were red. A bright, burning crimson. Gage squared his jaw and snapped the wallet shut, stuffing it back in his pants with a brusque gesture.

Calculus and Condoms

A spike of fear shot through Nathan that Gage might've clued into his true feelings. "What?" he snapped, sounding more defensive than he'd intended. "If you don't want people to see you're carrying rubbers, hide them better. Not that anyone gives a shit if you do or don't."

Gage rolled his eyes. "It's not that."

Too much frustration built up over time, coupled with nerves from what they were doing, pushed Nathan over the edge. "You have a problem with me being gay?" he fumed. "Just because I know you have condoms doesn't mean I'm going to want to fuck you."

"Where the hell did that come from?" Gage's face screwed up. "That has nothing to do with anything."

"Whatever," Nathan grumbled. "I still wouldn't do you, even if this does turn out to be the last night we spend on campus." He wedged the card into the narrow slit between the door and the jamb. He slid the plastic around, not knowing what the hell he was doing, but having seen enough movies to hope this dumbass trick would work. He regretted being out here with Gage now more than anything else and just wanted it to be over. Not because he was scared of getting caught breaking in, but more frightened with each second that he'd do something crazy like devour the man's lips in a passionate, open-mouth and all-tongue kiss that had to be illegal in most states, destroying what was left of their friendship in the process.

"Fuck!" he dropped the ID on the floor, giving up when the lock refused to pop. Gage had remained silent following his last outburst, and he reached out to try the handle. The door swung in.

"It was already unlocked," he said quietly, retrieving his ID.

Nathan went inside first. He'd started this damn thing—he might as well finish it. "Where does the guy file the shit for your class?" he asked, looking around the shadowy room.

Orange light from the sodium lamps outside the building filtered in through the blinds at the window, falling over a cluttered desk and a beat-up loveseat the professor must have pulled from the student lounge when the area was renovated last spring. Piles of ungraded exams and papers littered the floor. Nathan picked a stack at random and flipped through it.

"Hey, these are biology papers . . ." He frowned and tossed the stack on to the desk. "We're in the wrong office."

"I know," Gage said quietly, closing the door behind him. "I changed my mind about going through with it."

"But—" Nathan started.

"I want to you answer my question," Gage pressed, his gaze dropping to the floor. "Out in the hall, why did you say those things?"

Nathan shuffled in place. "It was nothing. Just forget it." He made for the door, but Gage grabbed his shoulders. The last thing he'd ever expected in a million years was for Gage to pull him into a kiss, but there he was, being drawn into the bigger man's embrace, a hot, searing mouth burning against his.

"I've wanted to do this for a long time." Gage pulled out of the lip-lock, breathing heavily. His loose-fitting jeans weren't so baggy now. A massive erection filled out the front of his pants like a pole in a tent. His hands dropped from Nathan's shoulders to settle over Nathan's ass instead, groping and kneading the muscle underneath the cotton sweatpants.

Nathan groaned, his legs spreading apart of their own will as Gage's fingers worked along the crack. Cloth rubbed against his anus, the friction sending a spasm of pleasure through Nathan's core.

"Shit," he gasped. He didn't know what was more shocking—the finger rimming his bunghole through his pants, or the fact that it was the untouchably hetero Gage doing it. Looking a gift horse in the mouth would, of course, be the stupidest thing to do on the face of the planet, so Nathan decided he'd go along with whatever Gage wanted. Hopefully, it involved being run through with that iron-hard rod stabbing up between Gage's legs.

"You know how many times I've jerked off thinking about you?" Gage breathed into Nathan's ear.

Probably not as many times as Nathan had. "Are you drunk, maybe?" He thought it was polite to ask, not that he had any actual intention of stopping regardless of the answer. He flicked his tongue over Gage's lower lip before licking his way inside that hot, welcoming mouth. Not a single trace of alcohol tinged the meaty, decidedly Gage-flavored taste as his tongue explored the moist depths.

Gage kissed him back with lip-numbing intensity. While their tongues clashed together, tasting, feeling, his mouth worked over Nathan's to pull, tug and suckle on lips dulled through sensory overload. The guy could kiss. Hard. The way a man could do only with another man.

Gage ended the kiss with a wet suctioning sound. His hands squeezed Nathan's ass, that one finger still nestled in the crack at the rim of Nathan's opening. His erection ground into Nathan's abdomen. "I need to know if you meant what you said before. That you don't want to fuck me."

"I was full of shit," Nathan barely recognized the sound of his own husky voice. Living with Gage for more than two disappointingly chaste years had been pure torture. He couldn't put into words how badly he ached for Gage. He didn't have to bother; the way his cock stiffened and jutted against Gage's hip had to say it loud enough.

"Why didn't you tell me anything?"

"I don't go after straight guys," Nathan swallowed. "It usually ends badly and I like having you as a friend."

"Considering you were willing to risk getting expelled for my sake, I don't think having sex would ever be enough to kill our friendship." The bright red blush returned to Gage's cheeks, visible even in the dim light. "Besides, who said I was straight?"

Nathan finally caught on. Gage's lack of girlfriends, his embarrassment when Nathan saw the condom, the repressed attraction . . . Gage had both feet in the closet, but Nathan had torn the door off its hinges and only needed to pull the man out.

He grabbed the back of Gage's neck. He trailed kisses down the slope of that handsome, freckle-dotted nose and over the sharp lines of his chin, where the first traces of stubble scratched at his lips. Rocking his hips, he drove the hard jut of his restrained erection against Gage's body, anxious for the moment they'd rip at each other's clothing.

"Fuck me already," Nathan rasped, yanking his shirt off over his head.

A groan of pure desire vibrated in Gage's chest. He finally released Nathan's ass to sweep over the span of naked torso. He spread out those big, thick-knuckled hands over Nathan's abs, feeling the ripples of muscles as he swept up towards Nathan's pecs.

God, those hands felt good. Rough and strong, encouraging Nathan to push against them while he rubbed Gage's back. The tension in those hard muscles yielded to his strokes, but when he slipped his fingers under the hem of Gage's T-shirt, Gage arched his back, his body tense again.

"It's okay," Nathan soothed. He moved his hands further up and around, caressing the hot skin along Gage's abdomen. He swept up, rolling the shirt out of his way as he went. He found

Gage's wide brown nipples and teased the nubs with thumb and forefinger. Gage let out a shuddering gasp. His nipples hardened into sharp peaks, beads of sweat dotting the cleft of his chest.

Nathan leaned in to lap at those droplets. The masculine taste slammed into his senses, spiking his arousal. He groaned, his cock so hard now it fucking *hurt*. He felt the trickle of pre-come already oozing from the head of his dick, his piece throbbing in time with his pulse. Setting both of his hands over Gage's, he coaxed his friend down to touch his cock straining against his clothes.

"It's all yours." Nathan thrust into the man's palms.

Swallowing loud enough for the gulp to be audible, Gage yanked down Nathan's sweatpants. He fondled the ball sack, separated now only by a thin layer of underwear. A little more comfortable now, but still achingly confined in those damn briefs, it felt like Nathan was never going to come. He whimpered, his prick pulling on the stretchy cotton like it might tear through the clothing in its eagerness to rest in Gage's sweaty palms.

"Hey," Gage stopped rubbing. "These are my briefs."

Nathan's breath locked in his throat. Oops.

"Heh," he managed a dry chuckle. There was no way he could confess to raiding Gage's laundry pile several times a semester, let alone admit that he'd masturbated with the stolen underwear. He'd wrapped this very pair of red briefs around his fist once and pumped his cock like there was no tomorrow. They'd absorbed the spray of come pretty damn well, at that.

Gage raised an eyebrow at him, but Nathan silenced any further comments by fixing his lips over a firm nipple and sucking. Hard. His tongue flicked over the peak as he sucked, and Gage started moaning with an intensity that would've put a seasoned porn star to shame. The noise struck a chord deep inside Nathan's gut that spiraled straight to his cock. He shivered and almost spurted on himself. It took a helluva lot of self-control to hold back the rush of jizz.

No more time to waste. Nathan pulled away from Gage's swollen nipple and finished yanking the underwear down. His cock bounced up, defying gravity in ways that just weren't possible without lust for another man to provide the lift.

Gage didn't fool around anymore either. As soon as Nathan's dick and balls were free, his hands were all over them. He cupped and squeezed and stroked and pulled, all at once. Nathan's knees went weak and he clutched at Gage's neck to keep from dropping into a writhing, orgasm-wracked heap.

Those hands moved to grip his ass, lifting Nathan off the floor. He was half-carried, half-thrown on to the couch where the smell of stale, old popcorn and dust greeting him. Gage leaned over the couch, one hand clutching the backrest. He jerked away the knotted mess of underwear and sweatpants so they bunched around Nathan's ankles, allowing freer access for both men.

And Nathan flaunted it. He lifted his dick and held the swollen slab at its base, his other hand cupping his sack. He trailed a finger down his scrotum, tracing the sensitive seam so he squirmed and gasped. When he reached the flexing hole between his ass cheeks, he shoved two fingers in and scissored the ring open. The muscle stretched and he let out a throaty groan at the friction, but he wanted to be ready. Nathan pulled out, slowly, a spasm running through the muscles in his passage.

Gage liked what he was seeing, obviously. The mound at his crotched swelled up, the outline of his penis creating a deep shadow in the strained denim.

Nathan propped himself up on one elbow and stroked a hand over Gage's erection. Judging from how hard and responsive the man's cock was, it was a miracle Gage hadn't creamed himself by now. Nathan invited himself to open the top button of Gage's pants.

"Oh, God," Gage moaned as Nathan worked the zipper next. The same shudder of anticipation that seized Gage's body ran through Nathan's. As soon as the metal teeth pulled apart, Nathan reached in, his fingers working into the seam of Gage's briefs. Burning hot skin welcomed him, and when he tried to close his hands around the shaft, his fingers just barely managed to circle the width.

Now Nathan was the one moaning. He tugged Gage's massive cock free, the heavy piece dwarfing whatever he'd fantasized about during those late-night hand jobs. He'd gotten one thing right, though: Gage was circumcised. He stared, still gripping the shaft in his trembling fist, his gaze swathing the entire length of shaft from the flushed tip to the root surrounded by a bed of dense black curls. A string of pearly white fluid trickled from the slit, while a vein wrapped around the cock like a thick, throbbing cord. Blood surged through the length, turning it a deep shade of red. Nathan gave that stunning prick a slow, hard stroke. A wad of hot come shot out and splattered across his cheek.

"Oh, fuck," Gage panted, charmingly awkward in spite of the way he kept on humping Nathan's palm. "I'm sorry."

"As long as you clean it up, I don't mind." Nathan sat up just enough so his lips could reach Gage's swollen, wet glans. He breathed along the slit before planting a soft kiss on the very tip.

Gage dipped forward, pushing Nathan back down on to the sofa. He lapped his tongue over the sticky mess streaking Nathan's cheek, drinking in his own spunk and hovering so close that beads of sweat spilled off his nose and onto Nathan's forehead. His hard cock dug into Nathan's abs.

Time to bury that rod somewhere else.

Nathan reached into Gage's back pocket for the wallet and the condom inside. A moment later, he had the wrapper off and the lubricated rubber out, and he was shoving Gage back to give them room. They fumbled together for a bit, both men forgetting how in the hell a condom is supposed to go on in their enthusiasm. They snorted with breathless laughter, using their clumsy groping as an excuse to keep touching and teasing each other. The rubber just barely made it to the root of Gage's cock, but it was enough.

Nathan rolled over onto his knees. He faced the back of the sofa and clutched the worn midnight blue cushions as he arched his back. His ass pointed out to Gage, his hole open and ready, gaping in the still air of the room. Two hands gripped his hips, holding them steady as the rounded knob of Gage's dick pressed on the opening.

"Do it!" Nathan rammed back into that rod. The rock-hard shaft drove into him, sliding on the slick coating of lube on the rubber.

Gage's cock filled him too much and too fast. Nathan's passage rolled against the fat piece of meat as it stretched to make the cock fit. His erection wilted for a second as the blood rushed straight to his head in that moment of sharp discomfort and fear. He cried out, but the pain was already spiraling into intense pleasure as Gage pegged him right in that sweet spot deep inside the canal. He moaned, his hips bucking to keep up with the feverish pace of Gage's thrusts. Sweat poured off Nathan's forehead, trickling down his naked torso. He twitched and writhed, his body held down by the sheer weight of Gage bearing down on him, his legs tethered by the jumble of clothes at his ankles. His cock kicked up again, the erection bigger and harder this time.

"You feel so good," Gage moaned. He pounded harder, until it felt as though a pile driver was grinding its way up Nathan's ass to mash at every single pleasure point in his passage. A burst of erotic pleasure knifed him deep in his groin, and nothing in the world could've stopped him from coming. Jizz sprayed out of him in an uncontrollable gush, splattering the back of the sofa in a burst of cream.

"Shit!" Gage sucked in a sharp breath, a shudder coursed through his body. He let out a choked scream and the condom ballooned inside Nathan. He kept thrusting, his balls smacking against Nathan's ass, until they both emptied. They climaxed again, the orgasm dry, but no less satisfying.

Exhausted, both men collapsed onto the sofa. The old lounge smells had been replaced with the rich, spicy odors of sweat and splooge. Nathan loved that smell. He wanted to be drenched in it again, this time in their dorm room, with Gage's naked body sandwiching him against the mattress.

"Should we clean this up?" Gage asked, his voice hoarse from the exertion. He fingered the ejaculate drying on the back of the sofa by Nathan's ear.

"It's so dirty already, I don't think it matters," Nathan chuckled. Besides, who could guess how many other students had already fucked each other senseless on the couch during the furniture's tour of duty in the lounge? His laughter died. "But what are you going to do about your calc class?"

"I'll take it next semester," Gage kissed the back of Nathan's neck. "I don't mind sticking around campus another six months as long as I have someone to spend the time with."

"Sweet," Nathan whispered. He smiled into the sofa. "We'll need more condoms."

Pledge Class

Neil Plakcy

I joined the rest of Lambda Phi Ro's freshman pledge class as we lined up in the living room of the frat house. There were six of us, starting with Rusty O'Brien, a linebacker on the freshman football squad, six-four, broad-shouldered and red-haired. At five-eight, skinny but fast on my feet, I was the smallest of the bunch, the pledge class's token geek—the one they expected to help them with their homework for the next four years.

The other brothers spread themselves around the living room on chairs, sofas, and the floor. For this final night of Hell Week, attendance was mandatory. Plus they all seemed to enjoy seeing pledges go through the kind of crap they'd gone through themselves.

All six of us were tired, mentally and physically. We'd been sent on scavenger hunts around the campus, yelled at, forced to clean the frat house from top to bottom, and criticized for everything from our taste in music to our choice of major. Rusty O'Brien had been ribbed for keeping a teddy bear given to him by a high school girlfriend, while the brothers had teased me for wearing boxer shorts that looked like they'd been handed down from my grandfather.

The goal of Hell Week was to break us down as individuals, and force us to learn to live with and work with each other as brothers. Just like in military training, the goal was to beat us up so much we had no choice but to rely on each other.

The pledge master was a skinny guy from New Jersey named

Eddie Pratt. "For your final activity in Hell Week, we've got something very special lined up for you," he said, standing in front of us, wearing jeans and a Lambda Phi Ro T-shirt. "First of all, take off your clothes. You won't need them for this."

We looked at each other, shifting around a little uncomfortably. Rusty, our unacknowledged leader, shrugged and started unbuttoning his shirt. Within minutes, all six of us were stark naked, our clothes in haphazard piles on the sofa.

I tried to pretend it was just like stripping in the locker room. I wasn't that much of an athlete, but I did like to swim, and I was accustomed to that time before and after each meet when guys were naked together, skinning into or out of Speedos. It was late fall, and the breeze blowing in through the open windows of the frat house was cool, raising goose bumps on my skin.

There were the obligatory catcalls. "You call that a dick, Lansing?" one guy said to me. "I call it a cocktail weenie." Everybody laughed except me; I blushed fiercely.

Another noticed that Craig Harkman had a budding hard-on. "The other guys turn you on, Harkman?" he said. "We'll be watching out for you in the showers."

A third razzed O'Brien for his hefty size. "Jesus, Rusty, you've got a promising career in porn."

A fourth added, "Yeah, gay porn," and the brothers all laughed.

Each of us had been assigned a big brother, and Eddie Pratt called them forward. Mine was a Chinese doper named Chuck Wei, and we hadn't exactly bonded, though he did have some pretty good pot, which he was willing to share. Each big brother had a coil of rope. "Stick your arms out in front of you, hands together," Pratt told us. "Your big brothers are going to tie your hands together."

There was a solemnity to the rite, despite the fact that all six of us holding our hands out were buck naked. Somewhere down Frat Row somebody was playing rap; somebody else battled it with reggae. Outside we heard a girl laughing and a dog barking.

The Lambda Phi Ro house was on the end of Frat Row, with a high wooden fence around the back yard, giving us more privacy than any other house. Pratt led the six of us, our hands tied together, through the kitchen and out the back door. The structure in the backyard looked like a boxing ring, with waist-high inflated rubber walls, kind of like the bottom half of a kids' bounce house. Next to the ring was a picnic table stacked with industrial-sized cans of vegetable oil.

"Pledges inside the ring," Pratt said.

We all looked at it. There was no entrance gate. "You may need the help of your big brother," Pratt added.

Rusty O'Brien stepped up to the ring and tried to lift his right leg over the rubber wall. He miscalculated, though, and ended up flat on his ass in the grass. The brothers got a good laugh out of that.

Craig Harkman took a running leap, trying to scissor kick over the wall, but ended up going over it head first. At least he was inside. He raised his tied hands in a gesture of victory and danced around.

The big brothers stepped up. Harkman's brother helped O'Brien's brother, since the football player was such a hefty package. "Hey, get your hand out of my ass," Rusty said, as the two boys lifted him up.

"Fist him," one of the other brothers called.

Chuck Wei basically picked me up at the waist and tossed me over the side, where I landed on top of Rusty O'Brien. It was comical to watch the two of us try to stand up without using our hands, and without touching each other anywhere that might cause the brothers to laugh. But I had to admit it was pretty erotic rubbing up against Rusty like that, both of us naked and in front of an audience. I struggled to think about math problems to keep my dick from swelling.

During the next few minutes, the big brothers managed to hoist and push the pledges over the side into the rubber pit. Fortunately the inflated floor and the walls gave when we bounced against them, so nobody broke any bones. "All right, line up again," Pratt told us.

We lined up as ordered, facing the brothers. "Big brothers, prepare the oil," he said.

Each of the big brothers picked up one of the huge jugs of vegetable oil, uncapped it, and began splashing it on the pledges. Chuck yawned as he was splashing me, and most of the oil ended up on the floor, not on me. "Get them good and oiled up," Eddie said. "They're going to need it."

A few minutes later, all of us naked pledges were dripping in oil. Oil had spilled on the rubber floor and the walls as well.

"Now for the blindfolds," Pratt said. Each big brother stepped up to his pledge and tied a blindfold around our eyes.

It was a really weird sensation. With my vision shut off, I could feel my body that much more, feel the oil dripping down my chest, pooling in the crack of my ass. It felt slippery and sticky and I yearned for a good, long shower to wash it all off.

"We're almost ready," Pratt said. "I hope you guys are going to put on a good show for us." The rest of the brothers laughed. "You all know what a circle jerk is, right? A bunch of guys get together and jerk off, and the first guy to spurt wins. Well, this is the Lambda Phi Ro version of a circle jerk. You can't use your hands, but you can use anything—or anyone—to get yourself off. First guy to shoot wins."

We all stood there dumbly for a minute. What the hell, I thought. They want a show? I'll give them a show. I turned to face the rubber wall and started rubbing my dick against it. "Lansing goes for the wall," one of the brothers crowed. "There's a guy who's accustomed to jerking himself off."

The other brothers laughed. Meanwhile, I could feel around me that the other pledges got the same idea, knocking into each other as they struggled to get themselves up to the wall. In his typical stoner way, Chuck hadn't tied my blindfold very well, and as I tried to fuck the wall, it came a little loose. Out of one side, I could see Rusty O'Brien, who appeared to be sniffing the air, moving around the fellow pledges as if he was in search of something, or someone, in particular.

Sure enough, he ended up right behind me. Raising his arms over my head and dropping them down around my neck, he got me locked in place. "Hey, what are you doing?" I asked.

"Winning," Rusty said. He positioned his dick against my ass and started rubbing.

It was like my whole body had turned into one big nerve ending. The combination of the blindfold, the oil, and Rusty's dick against my ass sent vibrations going from toes to fingertips—with special emphasis on my dick.

"Woo-hoo, look at O'Brien go," one of the brothers said, as Rusty ran his big sausage up and down my ass crack, getting it hard and lubed up.

"Jesus, who knew that dick could get any bigger," another marveled, as Rusty's dick swelled against my ass. Even though I was loving the feeling, I knew I had to at least pretend to fight back.

"Get off me, you big homo," I said, trying to buck back against the football player. But I couldn't match his size or strength, and actually my efforts just succeeded in helping his dick find my hole and plunge in.

"We have penetration!" a brother cried. Out of the corner of my blindfold, I could see him leaning down to look closely at Rusty's dick slamming into my ass.

This wasn't quite the way we'd rehearsed. Rusty was bigger than he'd ever been before, and he was fucking me faster, and harder, too.

I howled in pain. "You're splitting me open!" I cried.

"Yeah, that's what my girlfriend said last week," another brother wisecracked.

"The man's a fucking machine," Pratt marveled. With his clasped hands around my neck, Rusty had me locked in place. He pistoned his ass muscles, clenching and unclenching them, as he slammed his dick up my chute.

The great thing about having a stoner for a big brother was that he couldn't keep a secret. A couple of days before, Chuck Wei had spilled the beans about the final event of Hell Week. "They want to see who buttfucks who," Chuck had said. "You know, kind of like watching a dogfight. Who's the top dog in this pledge class?"

He giggled. "It's fucking hot, too," he said. "Most of the brothers won't admit it, but they get turned on watching a guy taking it up the ass. You'll see, as soon as it's over, everybody clears out. They all go fuck their girlfriends to prove to themselves that they're straight."

I got as many details about the oil challenge as I could before Chuck nodded off, and then I went directly over to Rusty's room at the dorm where the freshman football players were housed to tell him.

I found him sprawled on his single bed, wearing only a pair of loose athletic shorts. One of his balls had fallen out the side, and he scratched it as I explained the situation. "You're shitting me," he said, when I finished.

"Cross my heart and hope to fry," I said.

I'd met Rusty during the first week of school. We happened to sit next to each other in Calculus I, which I'd aced in high school, and, peering over at my results on the diagnostic exam we took that first day, he saw that I knew my stuff. Within a couple of weeks we had our own little ritual going: cocks and cosines. I'd tutor him for a while, then I'd suck his dick as he finger-fucked my ass. Just before he came, he'd start stroking me, and we'd both end up happy.

He was especially happy that he aced the first test, with my help. When he decided to pledge Lambda Phi Ro, he invited me along. Since then, we'd had a lot of fun together, though the one thing he hadn't done was fuck me. His dick was just too big.

When it comes to dicks, there are growers, and there are showers. The growers are guys like me. My dick's pretty average, based on my informal survey of locker rooms and porn mags. When limp, it's just a couple of inches. But when I get hard, and the blood vessels start pumping, I get up to about six and a half or seven inches.

Showers, on the other hand, are big boys, who don't get much bigger when they stiffen up. Rusty was a shower. Even when he wasn't excited, his dick was massive, too fat to wrap my hand all the way around and as long as a freshly sharpened number-two pencil. I knew there was no way I could get that meaty sausage up my narrow little ass chute.

"I should fuck you," I suggested.

Rusty laughed. "I got three words for you, pal. No. Fucking.

Way." He stood up and dropped his shorts. That big fuck stick stared out at me from a thatch of reddish pubic hair. "Maybe we ought to get some practice in before the big event."

I started to regret running immediately to Rusty with my news. "You can't fuck me, dude," I said, trying to reason with him. He turned his back to me as he bent over his desk drawer, looking for something.

His ass was damned near perfect. Two big round globes, with just a line of that red hair running between them. I'd licked him and tongue-fucked him and once he'd even let me fuck him, and I wanted more. "Come on, Rusty," I said, going over to him. I put my hands on his ass and started massaging, knowing that he liked the feeling of my fingers on him.

He turned around, holding a tube of grease in his hand, which he started massaging onto his dick. "Larry, baby," he said, leaning over to kiss me. "We all know the way it goes. I'm the football jock, you're the math geek. I fuck you. If I let you fuck me in front of all those guys, they'd never let me forget it."

I could have argued some more, but Rusty's chest against mine was driving me wild, and when he began rubbing his thumb over my lips I knew I was done for. I turned around and bent over. "Just don't do any permanent damage," I said.

Rusty was surprisingly gentle. He took his time, lubing my hole, finger fucking me with first one, then two digits, getting me loose. "Take a deep breath, baby," he said, and as I did I felt the head of his big dick pressing against my hole.

That whole deep breathing thing is a crock, by the way. When a guy as big as Rusty O'Brien starts to fuck you, you can breathe all you want and it's still going to hurt like a bastard. I felt all my nerve endings cluster around my ass, and every thrust sent waves of pain throughout my body.

Pledge Class

"Ow! Shit, that hurts," I said. But Rusty wouldn't stop. I kept moaning, and I even started to cry a little bit. But he didn't stop, and after a couple of minutes I started to get into it. He was going slow, being careful, and then I stopped crying and didn't mind all those sensations back there, because they were starting to feel pretty damn good. Rusty kept up a steady patter, too. "Man, that feels good," he said. "Your hole is so tight, Larry. Better than any pussy."

I didn't even have to touch myself; I came just after Rusty shot his load up my ass. And it was the most amazing orgasm, too.

Of course, we practiced a couple more times, but the frat kept us pretty busy during Hell Week, and we still had to go to class, eat, and all that other time-wasting stuff.

Our practice really paid off that night in the ring. The other pledges weren't having much success. From the corner of my blindfold, I could see that two of them didn't even have hard-ons, and the other pair were almost listlessly rubbing their flaccid dicks against the oily rubber walls.

Rusty O'Brien grunted with every thrust up my ass, and I kept on howling and whimpering, waiting for the moment when that pain would turn into pleasure. "Lookit, Lansing's crying," one of the brothers said, and I realized I was. "Man, O'Brien must really be fucking him."

The brothers of Lambda Phi Ro were enjoying the spectacle. I could see that more than a few were stroking hard dicks through jeans, and a couple even had hands down inside their waistbands. "This is better than blue movie night, because this is live and in person," I heard one of the guys say.

Finally those good feelings took over. I started to enjoy the fucking, and the audience, even bucking my ass back against Rusty a couple of times.

"Look at them go," one of the brothers said. "Lansing must have an asshole the size of the Holland Tunnel, the way he's swallowing O'Brien."

"We gotta get a video camera for next year," another brother said.

I began to pant, my breath coming in quick, shallow bursts, as I felt my whole body tense up for orgasm. I could feel that Rusty was ready too, and he howled as he backed his dick out of my ass, ready to explode. But before he could, streams of white jism spurted out of my dick. "We have a weiner!" Pratt shouted, even as Rusty's dick exploded onto my ass.

"I won!" O'Brien shouted.

"No, you didn't," Pratt said. "Your fuck buddy beat you by a couple of seconds." Everybody laughed.

The other four boys stopped what they were doing, figuring that the event was finished. "It's not over till it's over," Pratt said. "I think your big brothers need to show you how it's done."

Rusty's big brother, and Chuck Wei, untied us, took off our blindfolds, and helped us out of the ring. My ass felt like somebody had jammed a baseball bat up there, and I could hardly raise my leg enough to get over the rubber railing.

The big brothers of the other four boys stripped down themselves and stepped into the ring, coating themselves with vegetable oil.

"OK, boys, fuck 'em till they come," Pratt said. Each of the four big brothers led his charge to one side of the ring, leaned him up against the wall, and started fucking his ass, simultaneously reaching around and jerking his charge.

The two guys who didn't have hard-ons got there fast, and then it was a race to see which of the four pairs would get off first. I sat down on the ground, but my ass hurt so much I had to roll over onto my side. Rusty sat down next to me. "Sorry if I hurt you," he whispered, as we watched the four couples fucking. "But I had to do it."

"You'll make it up to me," I whispered back, and for just a moment I saw a little bit of fear on the big redhead's face.

Craig Harkman was the last guy to finish, finally shooting off about a thimble full of come, and his big brother had to help him out of the ring. As Chuck had predicted, the brothers scattered as soon as the show was over, the ones who'd been watching on their way over to their girlfriends to relieve those aching hard-ons. Even the ones who'd just come probably felt the need to rub off that ass juice in some girl's pussy.

Rusty and I hobbled back to his dorm room, where we collapsed next to each other on his narrow bed. "We made it, brother," he whispered into my ear. "Hell Week's over."

I reached under Rusty's bed for the package I had stashed there earlier in the week, pulling a huge rubber dildo out of the wrapping. It was even bigger than Rusty's dick, and that was saying a lot.

"You've got it wrong, brother," I said, pushing the beefy football jock over on his stomach and reaching for some lube for the massive dildo. "Hell Week is just starting for you."

Weekend Gig at State: or, The Night I Met Big D

Paul A. Cooper

I never had the pleasure of belonging to a fraternity. Hell, I never even went to a proper college.

When I graduated from high school, I had to go to work. My father was of the opinion that when you were finished with high school, you moved out of the house. So, that's what I did. I found myself a decent job, enrolled in junior college and spent nights playing in a band that I'd started with some friends a few months earlier. We practiced nearly every weeknight and would usually have a modest-paying gig on the weekends at some party or another. Music was my passion at the time, so it didn't matter that we barely made enough to get to the gig and back. Just playing in front of people was thrilling and, to be perfectly honest, I'd have done it for free.

While I was denied a proper college education, my best friends, Moochie and Dale, went away to State, where they both pledged and were invited to join the same fraternity, the name of which I will not reveal. They would call me every weekend and go on and on about the fun—or debauchery—that went on in their house. I was envious and wished that I had had the means to join them on their adventure. They told me that as soon as I had a free weekend, I should drive up and party down with them and their frat brothers. I agreed and told them that I looked forward to it.

It was just a couple of weeks later when I got a call from Moochie. Their frat was having the last big house party of the semester and they wanted me and my band to come up and play at the party. They couldn't pay, they said, but there would be plenty of free booze and we were promised one hell of a party. I immediately got on the phone with the rest of the band. We all agreed that it would be a blast, not to mention the exposure. Playing this party could open up more opportunities for us at other fraternity or sorority parties. I called Moochie back and told him we'd be there.

"You won't regret it," he said, and hung up.

A week later, we pulled up to the frat house in our U-Haul. We were welcomed and treated like royalty as several guys came out to help us unload and set up our gear. I spent some time catching up with Moochie and Dale, hearing more tales of the insane antics that went on in this house. We were introduced to most of the brothers and before long it was as if we were all long-lost friends. There seemed to be an endless supply of pizza, beer and Jell-O shots, all of which we sampled more than once. As the hours passed, more and more people were showing up. By about eight o'clock the place was packed and we were ready to go on.

We tore into our set—which, if memory serves, consisted of lots of R.E.M. and The Cure covers with a few originals thrown in—and the place was going nuts. They loved us. It was during our third or fourth song that I noticed this big guy inching his way through the crowd and closer to me. Dressed in cut-off blue jeans and a T-shirt with the sleeves ripped off, this guy was banging his head and singing along to all the songs. He had a girl hanging off of him like they were attached, but he didn't seem to even know she was there. He just kept pushing forward until he was standing right in front of me, banging his beer-filled fist in the air.

Weekend Gig at State

The more I watched him, the more I was attracted to him. He was a huge, beefy guy. His neck was probably as thick as my leg. He was tan and had recently shaved his head. He was watching me with what seemed to be an intense interest, too, hooting at me and doing strange things with his tongue. I'm a decent-looking guy. Basic musician type, skinny with muscular arms, shoulder length dark hair and, I'm told, beautiful eyes. However, I've never been real comfortable with someone staring at me the way he seemed to be—but who was I to complain?

My eyes were scanning him, from his flip-flopped feet up his insanely hairy legs. He was barrel-chested and had quite an impressive bulge going on in his cut-offs; I wondered if this was because he was interested in me, or because of that little bitch gyrating up and down his side. I was thankful that I had a guitar to hide my now-growing crotch, and every now and then, I would press my guitar against myself, sending small pulses of pleasure through my body. I'm surprised that I could remember what chords to play.

About halfway through our normal set, it became clear that a couple of the guys in my band were no longer in any shape to play—not that many people in this crowd would have noticed. Still, we agreed to call it a night as far as the live music was concerned, and we cranked a tape deck through our PA system and began to head into the crowd to enjoy the festivities. I headed over toward the kegs, dodging groups of inebriated people drinking beer from a funnel. As I was filling my cup from the tap, I glanced across the room and noticed that the new object of my desire was against the far wall in conversation with my buddy, Dale. I headed their way.

"This is Eddie! One of my best friends for as long as I can remember," Dale said to the guy as he swung his arm around my neck. "Eddie, this is Derrick. He lives in the house. He was just tellin' me how much he enjoyed watchin' you play."

"Hi, Derrick," I said, shaking his hand. "I'm glad you enjoyed the show. What little show there was."

"You guys sounded great, and I love the way you play."

"Thanks," I said, blushing a little.

"Make sure Big D doesn't get out of control tonight," Dale said as he moved on to another group of people nearby.

"Who's Big D?" I asked

"You'll probably meet him later."

"Where's your girlfriend?" I asked.

"Ah, Jessica? She's not my girlfriend. Just some troll that hasn't left me alone since she got here. I think she spotted some of her friends and took off. Fine with me," he said as he finished his beer and steered me toward the keg.

We made small talk as he filled both of our cups. Derrick had this strange way of rubbing up against me while he talked. Maybe it was the beer, I'm not sure, but it was very erotic to feel his sweaty arms come into contact with my body every few minutes.

After we'd chatted for quite a while, Derrick said, "Follow me. You gotta see the basement." He opened a door off the kitchen and motioned me down some stairs.

"Okay," I replied, and started down as I heard him latch the door behind us.

As I entered the dark room, the smell hit me. It smelled a lot like my high school locker room, but with a hint of urine and spunk. Derrick walked around me and pulled a chain hanging in the center of the room and a single red light bulb came to life. I glanced around the room. A washer and dryer along one wall, with baskets of what appeared to be dirty laundry piled next to them. Derrick walked to the far wall and flipped on a stereo. He then walked over to a bucket in the corner and urinated in it. I was still trying to take all this in, becoming more and more aroused by the minute.

As I walked deeper into the room, I bumped into something that I hadn't seen. It was a makeshift bed made of what looked like cinder blocks and plywood, topped with a mattress that had seen better days.

"What's this for?" I asked.

Derrick walked over to me and said, "I'll show you." He gave me a slight push and I fell back onto the mattress.

The next thing I knew, he was straddling me, pushing my chest back down as I tried to sit up. He leaned until his face was inches from mine. I could feel his breath on my lips. He kissed me hard, briefly, before backing off.

"Do you mind that I did that?" He was staring directly into my eyes, a slight grin on his face. He already knew the answer.

My heart was racing now and my hard-on raging. "No," I said. "I don't mind at all."

He smiled wide. "I had a feeling you wouldn't mind."

Derrick reached down and pulled my shirt up and over my head, tossing it on the floor. He did the same with his, revealing his huge chest entirely carpeted with light-brown hair. I heard him kick his flip-flops to the floor as he leaned back down and kissed me again. This time, his massive tongue pushed through my lips and filled my mouth. I wrapped my arms around his massive body and pulled him closer to me. As we kissed, his hand slid down my chest and onto my jeans. He found my cock, by this time at full mast, and began rubbing it through my pants. I could feel my underwear getting moist as I pushed against his hand.

He climbed off of me and went to the foot of the bed. He removed my shoes and socks before reaching up and pulling my jeans and underwear off and throwing them to the floor. I now lay completely exposed, the single red light bulb swinging above me. I looked at Derrick. He unbuttoned his shorts and let them fall, revealing a jockstrap with a big wet spot and a huge purple knob sticking out the side. *I must be dreaming,* I thought. *Things like this just don't happen to me.*

"Eddie, Eddie, Eddie . . . ," he whispered as he ran his hands up and down my legs. "You're so fuckin' hot."

I said nothing.

Still standing at my feet, Derrick grabbed my calves and pulled me to the edge of the bed, letting my legs hang over the end. Then, without warning, he leaned down and took my aching prick in his mouth. Using his hand to guide it, he slid my pole in and out of his mouth, pausing to suck every drop of pre-come out of me. I gripped the edges of the mattress to steady myself. He knew how to suck a cock. This was not his first time. It was only my fear that someone would discover us that kept me from immediate orgasm.

With one last, hard suck, Derrick released my cock, stood up and said, "You enjoying yourself?"

"More than you can imagine," I said.

Derrick put his thumbs into the waistband of his jockstrap and slid it off, balling it up and laying it beside me on the mattress. His beer-can-sized dick stood at attention, adorned by an unkempt bush of brown hair. I watched, not able to take my eyes off him. He reached down and grabbed his massive, wet cock and started stroking it. With his free hand, he began rubbing my ass crack, prying my cheeks apart with his fingers before locating my hole. He touched it with his thumb, applying a good bit of pressure. He took his hand away, spat in it, then smeared his spit on my crack. As he continued to rub and squeeze his purple prick, I felt my barrier give way and his thumb was inside me, probing around. I shuddered and felt myself get chills over my entire body.

I leaned up on my elbows. "I'm not sure how you're gonna do it, but you need to get that cock inside me," I said.

Derrick looked at me and grinned. "This is Big D," he said as he smacked his cock against my leg. "He's very pleased to meet you."

"The pleasure's all mine," I said.

He lifted my ass a little, spread my cheeks and spat directly onto my asshole, rubbing it around with his thumb. He then spat in his other hand, using it to lube up his cock. I spread my legs a little more and Derrick moved forward, pressing the head of his meat against my hole. As he pushed, I grabbed my ass cheeks and spread them open as wide as I could. It felt as if someone was trying to drive a Buick up my ass.

"I don't know if it's gonna fit," I gasped.

"It'll fit," Derrick said, reassuringly. "Just be patient. It always fits."

And he was right. After concentrating and taking some deep breaths, my muscles relaxed and Derrick's beer can prick slid inside me.

"Oh, fuck!!!!" was all I could say. I felt as if I was being split open. But, at the same time, I wanted more. I reached back and grabbed him by his huge hairy cheeks, pulling him further into me. He responded by pounding me harder.

"Shit, Eddie. You feel so fucking good, dude," Derrick grunted as he slammed into me. He placed his palms on the balls of my feet, curled his fingers over my toes and shoved my legs back until my knees were touching my shoulders. "I'm gonna fuck you so good you won't ever wanna fuck anybody else," he said. He sped up his thrusts and I could feel his nut sack banging against my ass as his prick slid in and out of my hole.

I didn't want to touch my cock for fear that I would come. I reached down and started tugging on my scrotum, rolling my swollen balls around in my fingers. With my other hand, I was tweaking and twisting on my nipples.

"Oh, God!" I screamed as he hit my prostate extra hard, making me squirm in pleasure and pain. "That's it, Derrick. Keep fuckin' me just like that."

"That what you like, skinny boy?" he growled. "Big D's gonna tear that ass up!" And he wasn't kidding. He was tearing me up and I was loving every minute of it. "Yeah, boy! I'm gonna fuck that ass so hard you're gonna have to crawl out of here!"

"Oh, yeah?" I said, trying to breathe. "Give it your best shot, Big D. Show me how hard you can fuck me!" He increased his speed. "That's right. Harder!!" I gasped.

I looked down and saw his jockstrap still lying on the mattress beside me. I reached down and grabbed it, and, placing it over my nose and mouth, I took a deep breath. The scent was intoxicating and I just held it there as he continued to plow me. With the jockstrap still held to my face, I reached down and pushed my cock at the base, causing it to point straight up. On Derrick's next thrust, I lost control without even stroking my dick.

"Aaaaaaahhhhhhh!!!" I yelled as a steady stream of white liquid shot straight up in the air, hitting Derrick in the face and chest, dripping down him.

"Oh, yeah!" he said as he pummeled me. "Spray that shit all over Big D."

I began stroking my dick and was surprised when I had what seemed like a second orgasm, though not as strong as the first. "Oh, shit! Oh, shit!" I screamed as I continued to stroke until I could no longer take it.

Then, without warning, Derrick pulled his fat cock completely out of me, wrapped both hands around it and began beating it furiously. I stared in amazement at that big purple hunk of meat as he moaned and groaned, face blood red and sweat pouring off him.

"Oh, yeah, boy!" he growled through clenched teeth. "I hope you're ready for it cause Big D's gonna to hose you down!" He continued pounding, made a few wincing noises, then yelled, "Oh, boy! Yeah, here it comes. Big D's coming . . . Big D's coming . . . Yeeeeaaaahhhhh! Ooooohhhhhhh, Yeeeeeaaaaaahhhhhh!" And with that, he was flowing, his juice flying everywhere and covering me from head to toe. He squeezed until there was not a drop of fluid left in him. "That's what I'm talkin' about," he said, chest heaving and breath slowing. Slowly, he crawled up, pausing to lick a puddle of come off my chest. He pressed his member against mine and stuck his tongue in my mouth, sharing with me what he'd found.

When Derrick finally climbed off of me with his cock starting to droop, I was beyond exhausted. He tossed me a towel out of one of the laundry baskets, grabbed one for himself and we both began to wipe off the mess we'd made. I pulled my stiff, aching body up off the mattress, stood on wobbly legs and began to get dressed. Derrick walked over to the bucket in the corner and pissed again, before rounding up his clothes and putting them on. As we headed for the stairs, he paused and put his hand on my shoulder.

"That's some hot ass you got," he said.

"That's some hot cock you got," I replied, and headed back to the party upstairs.

I walked out of the basement on sore legs, barely able to stand. Derrick got each of us a beer, then he winked at me and headed back into the crowd. I looked around and finally spotted Dale and Moochie leaning against the back wall talking. I limped over to them, my hair still drenched in sweat, as both of them burst out in laughter.

"What's so funny?" I asked.

"Looks like you met Big D," Moochie said as they cackled.

I had nothing to say.

My band was a hit at State that night. As a matter of fact, nearly every weekend after, we would have a gig up there at one house or another. Many of those nights, I'd look down and there would be Derrick, right in front, his fist in the air and his tongue hanging out. And usually before the night was over, Big D and I would repeat our past adventure. And he had been correct. He fucked me so good, I never wanted to fuck anybody else.

Initiation Night

Rob Rosen

Initiation night—in a way, much the same as a Halloween: a lot of smoke and mirrors, a fear of what lurks around the corner, of the unknown, of people dressed in sheets looking to scare the shit out of you. The only difference being, perhaps, on Halloween you aren't forced to strip down to your boxers, especially while blindfolded, and especially on either side of a dozen other nervous guys. Throw in your hands tied at the wrists, and perhaps initiation night isn't so much like Halloween after all.

Then again, mine was, as it turned out, chock full of tricks and treats.

Looking back on it, I suppose I'd seen enough movies to expect what was going to happen. Still, with rampant nationwide hazing deaths, plus the subsequent lawsuits, my initiation night, as stated, really was just a lot of smoke and mirrors; and the sheets were more like robes, but with a similar effect: I was, despite it all, scared shitless.

I mean, yeah, the goldfish tasted remarkably like peaches going down; the sound of fuckable goats and sheep had that piped in quality; and the paddles never went wood to skin. Then again, being half-naked and cast in utter darkness is never much fun. Mostly. I mean, at first, anyway.

The night went on for what seemed like hours. Lots of pushing and shoving, veiled threats, hushed whispers, brothers who had too much too drink, pledges with not enough; and all with the promise that when the sun came up, you'd no longer be a lowly pledge.

It was the shared experience of that night that brought us together as brothers; something had all been through, going back decades. The ritual and the secrets were binding.

And so, theoretically, were our wrist restraints.

When the evening finally drew to a close, I was tossed into a room atop a scratchy blanket. My blindfold still hung precariously around my head. The torn fabric still held my hands together. And, it seemed, I was not alone. I could, quite clearly, hear breathing from across the room.

"God, that was endless," I said with an exhausted sigh.

"Greg? That you?" came the familiar voice, perhaps three feet in front of me.

"Yep," I replied. "Dave?"

"Yeah, dude."

I gulped, silently. I'd had little contact with Dave. He was class president. Blond, blue eyed, godly. The sorority girls giggled whenever he sauntered by. The guys all high-fived him, wanted to be him. A different species from me altogether. Strange we'd both pledged the same fraternity; stranger still to be locked in a room with him, and under those "circomestances."

Then silence. Breathing. A creak in the floorboards, a rumble in my belly. "Now what?" he eventually asked.

"Guess we go to sleep," I surmised.

"And wake up one of the chosen few." He laughed, derisively.

"What, isn't this what you wanted?"

The laughter abated. He paused, then told me, "Not really. I'm a legacy. My father pledged here back in the good old days. Guess I didn't have much of a choice."

The comment hung there, heavy all around us. Most guys I met would've killed to be a brother in my fraternity; and Dave fairly reeked of that frat guy mentality. Guess I'd been mistaken about him. Gee, the night was proving to be full of surprises. And that one was quickly followed by yet another, as I leaned my head against the wall behind me, and my blindfold at last came undone and fell silently to the floor.

I squinted ahead. Dave sat across from me, his legs spread apart, his hands tied as one, resting in his lap, his lean, hard body glowing in the moonlight that worked its way through the room's only window. Blond hairs rose densely up his well-worked calves and thighs, only to trickle up his deeply etched stomach as they petered out across his chiseled, tight chest. I could now smell him from across the room, the scent of sweat and beer drifting through the must.

I craned my head downwards, staring up the gap in his boxers, certain I'd never get a chance like this again. The tip of his prick poked out, white in the light, his piss slit just barely discernible. Again I gulped, my own prick growing rigid beneath the thin layer of cotton.

"Say something," he finally whispered. "Too quiet in here."

My mind went blank; then it went fucking haywire before finally landing on a worthwhile thought. "Um, were you ever a Boy Scout?"

"Why?" he asked. "They lock you up in your drawers there, too? Prepping you for this?"

I laughed. "No, but sort of. I mean, I learned how to tie knots. And untie them, too. So, sort of prepping me for this. In a weird kind of way, I mean."

"Go figure," he said with a chuckle. "So all hope is not lost. Goodie."

"You always this sarcastic, dude?" I asked, pushing myself up off the ground.

"Only when I'm locked in a room, naked and hogtied."

I stood over him and began to jiggle my fingers through my bindings. "Not naked," I corrected. "And hogtied would mean your feet as well as your hands."

He laughed with a snort. "Well now, look whose glass is half full."

Glass half full *and* hands untied. Guess that merit badge finally came in handy. I stared down at him as I pulled my prick out of my boxers and stroked myself just a scant few inches away, waving my growing woody in front of his impossibly handsome face. A bolt of adrenalin shot up my spine and my knees grew weak and wobbly.

"Untied yet?" he finally asked.

And then it was my turn to laugh. "It's hard," I replied. "The knot, I mean." Though, of course, I meant my cock, which by then was at its full seven arced inches, with a bead of pre-come dribbling over the helmet, reflecting the moonlight to my left. His mouth, now inches away, looked good enough to fuck.

"Well, hurry, I gotta take a piss."

I looked around and shook my head. "The bathrooms are down the hall, dude."

"Then pray there's a jar in here somewhere."

The thought quickly withered my prick, which I reluctantly stowed away. "There," I eventually said. "Untied." And then I bent down and removed his blindfold. He looked up at me, our faces now up close and personal, his eyes beaming beneath the dim glow. My cock bounced but otherwise stayed put. This sort of thing they didn't teach you about in the Boy Scouts. Too bad.

"Um, whenever you're ready, you can untie me, please," he said, still all smiles.

A red flush crept up my neck and spread across both cheeks, hidden, gratefully, by the semidarkness of the room. "Oh yeah," I said, sitting back down in front of him as he held his wrists up for me. My hands brushed his, flesh on flesh, sending a warm shiver across my back. I twisted and tugged at the material. Sadly, it wouldn't give, as mine had. "The knot's too tight," I informed.

"Not good," he groaned.

"Sorry," I apologized, again looking up at him and then quickly back down.

"No, I mean, *not good.* I really do have to piss."

I looked around. The room was fairly barren, save for our two blankets and some dusty boxes. Then I looked towards the window. "Out there," I suggested. "Better than in here, anyway."

I jumped up and helped him to his feet. He tilted and swayed, his lean body colliding with my own, rubbing against me for the briefest of ecstatic moments before he righted himself and walked to the window, which I quickly opened for him.

"Houston, we have a problem," he then proclaimed. I watched as he tried unsuccessfully to extract his prick from his boxers, and then just as unsuccessfully to yank them down. "Fuck," he finally shouted. "You're gonna have to help me out here."

I coughed and wiped a newly formed bead of sweat from my brow. "If by *help* you mean shut the window and cover you with the blanket, all nighty-night like, then fine. Otherwise, the Boy Scouts have strict rules against abetted peeing."

"Look," he said, shifting from foot to foot in obvious agony. "Just pull down my drawers; I'll do the rest."

I feigned revulsion, but then quickly stood behind him. "Not a word of this to anyone," I told him, crouching down as I tugged his boxers to the ground, my face achingly at ass level as I stared longingly at his hair-lined crack and perfect alabaster cheeks.

"Trust me," he said. "This ain't no Hallmark moment for me either."

I stood up and moved away, my eyes still taking in his virtually naked frame, too nervous, at least, to pop yet another boner. And then I waited. And waited. And waited some more. "Well?" I asked.

"I can't go with you standing back there like that."

I laughed. "Well, considering we're in a room that's ten by ten, and locked inside to boot, I'd say you have little choice. Besides, you pee next to guys all the friggin' time."

"*Next* to guys, yes. Not with guys standing right behind me who aren't peeing."

Which, of course, left me few options. "Fine," I said, walking up and standing by his side before kicking off my boxers and aiming my prick out the window. Soon enough, I was sending a yellow stream to the ground below. And then, shortly thereafter, so was he.

"Thanks," he said. "That was very *brotherly* of you."

"Yeah, well, I have a brother at home, and this is something we've never done together. But you're welcome."

We stood there like that, pissing in unison, as I tried my best not to stare down at his distractingly close schlong—which was odd, because I had the distinct feeling that he was staring at mine. When I looked to my side to confirm this, that is just what I found. "Um," he said, "you're, uh, not circumcised."

I stared down at my prick and grinned. "Guess I prefer the turtle-necked variety." I pointed to his. "As opposed to the short-collared one. Why, haven't you ever seen foreskin before?"

He shook the last vestiges of urine from his dick, and replied, "Truly a night of firsts." And then, strangely, he kept on shaking it. And tugging. And pulling. I watched in rapt amazement as it grew and grew, quickly thickening to six fat inches that pointed straight up and out. "Sorry, I can't sleep if I don't pop a load off beforehand."

An anxious tic pulled at my cheek. "So you can't pee with me behind you, but you can jack off with me next to you? Dude, you are a weird one."

He released the beast and pointed to my own. "Hey, your sleeve is shrinking. Cool."

I grinned. "Um, yeah, it does that when the rest of me, uh, *grows*." I looked away, and quickly added. "I mean, I thought it would make you more comfortable if I shot one, too."

He chuckled, and said. "Hey, Greg, can I tell you something?"

I turned my head and stared into his sparkling blue eyes, which bore right on through me, laser intense. "Yeah?" I squeaked out.

"When two guys stand next to each other with hard-ons, pounding their puds, it ain't out of consideration."

"No?" I asked, my hands now fairly trembling.

"No," he replied, his voice raspy, his face leaning over and into mine. "So why don't you just kiss me already?"

I stared at him, confused, dumbfounded, and super horny—not necessarily in that order. "Uh, are you testing me or something, dude?"

He answered by brushing his lips against my own, soft and gentle, caressing my mouth with his, before he slithered a wet tongue out and parted his way inside. And then he whispered into my mouth. "Yep, and you passed with flying colors."

Our mouths mashed together, his kisses growing insistent as he turned his body into mine and mine into his, until our cocks were pressed up as tightly as our faces, grinding together. I reached out and ran my hands down his slender back, playing with the fuzzy hair just above his rump, and then headed southward to splay his cheeks apart with my fingers, teasing the hair-rimmed hole nestled within. He moaned, softly, the sound rumbling over me like an avalanche.

And then, oddly, he laughed as I held him in my arms, nibbling on his neck as I made a beeline for a tender earlobe. "What's so funny?" I whispered.

"Well, you know before, when you were shaking that big dick of yours in my face?"

I gulped. "Oh, you, uh, saw that?"

"Oh, uh, *yeah*," he said, reaching his bound hands up to twist and tug on one of my nipples. "Not like the blindfolds were put on as well as these damned wrist restraints. Anyway, I wondered how long it would take before I got a taste of it."

I pulled away and again stared at his shimmering pools of blue. "But you haven't tasted it yet."

"Well, yeah. I bet myself it would take me ten minutes, though. And, based on my calculations, plus the watch on my wrist, I have about one minute to go."

I laughed and slapped him on his nearly smooth chest. "Then you better hurry, dude."

"Oh, yeah," he eagerly agreed, sinking to his knees and then taking my cock in his mouth, sending a million tingles eddying around my crotch before they shot in all directions. I grabbed the back of his head and coaxed my prick down his throat. He looked up at me, a lone tear trickling down his cheek as he gagged, contentedly, on my thick slab of meat.

"How do I taste?" I asked, caressing his scruffy cheek.

"Come down here and see for yourself," he told me, in between sucks and slurps.

I joined him on the floor and once more locked my lips on his, our eyes opened, staring ahead, locked on target. When I came up for air, I said, "Mmm, I taste good. Must be the extra skin."

He laughed. "Really? Maybe you need something to compare it to."

"Good idea, dude," I agreed. "On your back, please."

He did as I asked, lying on the blanket with his legs spread apart, his magnificent body spread out before me like a veritable buffet. I grabbed for his heavy nut sack and gave a tug, pulling his dick down as I aimed it for my mouth. In one fell swoop, I engulfed his thick prick while he wriggled and squirmed beneath me, his moans filling the small space around us. When I eventually popped it back out, he asked, "Well?"

"Oh man, you taste good. Almost as good as me."

He grinned as he stroked his billy club of a dick, his chest muscles constricting and relaxing as he moved his hand up and down. "*Almost*, huh?" he asked, with a wink. "Maybe this will even things up, then." His raised his knees up and rested his ankles on my shoulders. I stared down, hungrily eyeing his pink, crinkled hole, which also now winked up at me.

I bent down and took a deep whiff of him, of his musky center which beckoned me ever inward. My tongue darted out, licking its way upwards until it landed on the bull's-eye. His ass tasted of salt and sweat. I pushed his cheeks further apart and dove in, burying my tongue inside of him as I reached up to stroke his pulsing cock.

"Oh man," he sighed, only to repeat it, louder, as I slid a wetted finger up and in and back, feeling the silky smooth interior of him. "Yeah," he added. "Fuck that ass, dude."

My cock quivered at the sound of it, but unless the boxes around me were full of rubbers, which seemed unlikely, I opted for a second finger. He squirmed and sucked in his breath before relaxing his grip on my digits, and then he exhaled, deeply. "Okay?" I asked.

He nodded and grinned. "Try a third, dude. Three's the charm."

I spit on his hole and deftly entrenched the third and final digit, filling him up but good. And then in and out my fingers went, retracting with a *pop* before gliding in again, back, back, back to the farthest reaches of his ass. He bucked his rump and writhed on the blanket as I increased the pace up his chute, quickly working my fist to a fevered, pistoning pitch as I fucked his ass, just as he'd asked me to do.

"Go, Boy Scout, go," he rasped, his breath now jagged as I buried my fingers up his tight hole, feeling the familiar hardening of his prostate as I gave one last push and shove. With a final stroke of his fat cock, his body quaked and he erupted, spewing ounce after hot, molten ounce of thick, white come, which shot up and out, drenching his chin, his chest, and his rapidly rising and falling belly. His moans filled the small room, reverberating in my ears and rumbling through me like a runaway train. "Your turn, Greg," he finally said. "Quick, let's see you shoot."

I gently removed my fingers, hocked a loogie down at my cock, and began a quick jack at my steely cock, which by then was ready to blow; and then, shortly thereafter, did. My moans drowned out his, my head tilted back, and every muscle in my body went rigid as my cock exploded, shooting rope after rope of come, which mixed and mingled with his own before dripping over his sides.

Spent and sweat-soaked, I collapsed on top of him, praying that one of the nearby boxes had something inside of them that could clean up our sticky mess. Barring that, I was all for a tongue bath. In any case, my mouth quickly found his as our bodies slipped and slid and ground into one another.

When we finally came up for air, and with our cocks already rock-solid, I again stared into his sparkling eyes, blue as the sky on a hot summer's day. "Hey, *brother*," I said to him.

"Hey, *brother*," he echoed, with a mischievous grin. He paused and then leaned in for a deep, perfect kiss, and then asked, "By the way, were you planning on living in the house next year?"

I nodded. "Yeah, you?"

He nodded as well, then added, "You know the benefit of being the president of the pledge class, right?"

"Tightest wrist restraints?"

He laughed. "No, dude. I, um, I get to pick my roommate." Again he paused and shyly looked away for the briefest of moments. "You interested?"

My heart skipped a beat, but with a wide smile, I replied, "I guess I passed the initiation, then."

He returned my smile with one of his own. "Oh, dude, you passed. Man, you passed. In fact, I think we should start the ceremony all over again. If you're ready for round two."

I reached down and slapped my rigid cock against his. "Yeah, dude. Ring the fucking bell and *come* out fighting."

He laughed and stretched his arms around me in a big bear hug. "You know, if this is what they taught you in the Boy Scouts I think I missed out, big time."

"Don't worry, dude," I said, gently sucking on an eraser-tipped nipple. "I'll teach you everything I know. Every fucking thing."

Witi

Anthony Lectito

It had been a slow week so far. There had been just enough customers to warrant the boss keeping the shop open, but nowhere near enough to have me run off my feet. For many people, I'm sure it would have been considered a bit of a drag, certainly not the ideal way to spend a Friday evening, but it worked out well as far as I was concerned. It meant I had a ready-made excuse when the other guys inevitably decided they wanted to have a night out on the town, and as a bonus I was able to do some of my course readings during the quiet periods. I rarely had this kind of peace in the dorm, so Friday evenings became something of an escape for me. Every Friday evening, at around seven, I'd arrive at Better Books for the closing shift.

At that time of night there only needed to be one person on duty—on a Friday evening the only people we tended to get shopping were the hard-core bibliophiles, the lonely, or those killing time before heading to the nearest nightclub—none of whom were likely to cause too much trouble. When people walked through the door it became a bit of a game, anticipating what they would choose to buy, and guessing what their reading habits said about their sexual behavior. They ranged from the white-bread Nora Roberts fans to the more hard-core Anne Rice aficionados.

Julian, who shared a couple of classes with me, was one who caught my eye. When he started browsing the work of Witi Ihimaera, I knew he was going to be a challenge for me. I'd long been a fan of Ihimaera. Such hauntingly sensual writing, so poetic. Yet so angst-ridden, so conflicted. It had taken months of searching secondhand bookshops, but I'd gradually tracked down first editions of all his books. To see Julian looking through his books set my heart racing. I had to make the most of the opportunity.

"Have you read many of his books?" I asked. Clichéd, for sure, but that was to be expected.

"I haven't read any, yet. Is there anything you'd suggest?"

"Sure," I replied. "You've got to read . . ." Squatting down, I reached for a copy of the book, which I passed up to him, my fingers lightly brushing his as he took it from me. As I went to stand, I grabbed his arm to pull myself up, ending up standing close enough to him that he would be able to sense my interest.

As he leaned against the bookshelf he gave me a cheeky grin. "Have you got any favorite passages?" I knew I had him at that point, and put my hand on the shelf beside him. "If you can wait half an hour, we can go back to the dorm, I can show you my favorite passage . . ."

The half hour till closing time was the slowest I'd had for a long time, but we soon ended up back in my room.

My dorm is pretty much like any other dorm in the country. On the wall, myriad posters of various actresses, testifying to my roommate's latest infatuations. In the air, a faint tangy smell, suggesting it had been more than a few days since Phil, my roommate, had put a load of washing through the machine. Along one wall was Phil's bed, adjacent to his desk.

Along the other wall was my bed. It was here that I led Julian. "We've got a couple of hours before my roommate returns," I whispered, as I reached out to stroke Julian. I used my index finger, then my second finger, as I gently brushed down the side of his face; over his cheek, under his chin. Ever so lightly I ran my nails along his lips. As I traced around to his ear, to his sideburns, Julian tilted his head, snuggling his face into my palm. I knew he was mine for the taking. My hand—my left hand—worked its way through his thick mane to the back of his skull, and I spent a moment or two massaging the back of his head. Before long, I gripped his hair, taking a good handful of it, and pulled him towards me. All this time he stood limply, arms hanging by his side. He wasn't objecting to what I was doing, but nor was he initiating anything. Clearly he wanted me to take charge. I gripped his hair, pulling him towards me, stopping him when his lips were an inch from mine. I waited, gazing into his eyes, seeing if he could hold out, or if his desire would get the better of him. I timed my breath with his. As he breathed out, I breathed in. As he breathed in, I breathed out.

I darted my tongue out, allowing it to momentarily make contact with his lips, before pulling away. At this, Julian's composure cracked, and he leaned forward, eager to complete a kiss. With his hair still in my hand, I swiftly yanked back, pulling his head away from me. He squirmed a little, but soon realized I had no intention of letting him go. "No," I snapped, "not yet. You can wait until I'm ready." My eyes drilled into his, until he looked away in submission.

"Yes, sir." he meekly replied.

As he quietly stood, I moved around behind him. Gently wrapping my arms around him, I began nuzzling the back of his neck. My lips, my tongue traced their way along his collar, licking at the small droplets of sweat forming as he tried to restrain himself. I nibbled his ear, taking his earlobe between his teeth, biting it tenderly, pulling at it with my teeth. With my hands, I was slowly forging a path around his body, carefully avoiding anything that would give him too much of a thrill. I avoided his nipples, and his crotch, focusing instead on leaving him wanting more. I stroked his sternum, rubbed his stomach; gently held his hips and his thighs. More than enough to get him worked up and excited, but leaving him frustrated.

As I reached up to undo the top button on his shirt, my wrists brushed his nipples, and he let out a gasp. "You like that, don't you?" I muttered in his ear, reaching into his shirt and giving his nipples a tweak.

"Yes," he replied, his voice panting, revealing the extent of his desire, his body leaning back against mine. I undid another button on his shirt. Then another. Before long, his shirt was open, exposing his chest and stomach to the air. Smooth, almost hairless, his torso played with the low light in the room, the ridges of his stomach exaggerated by the gentle shine from the lamp on my desk. Below his navel was a thin trail of dark hairs, leading to his waistband, almost as though leading the way for future explorations. On each side of his chest were faint circles of hair, cushioning two very erect nipples. Whether they were responding to the cool night air, or were simply reflecting Julian's state of arousal, they were demanding my attention. I trailed my right hand up Julian's body. Up his stomach, over his sternum, his throat, his chin. I paused for a moment at his lips, before plunging thumb and a finger into his mouth. "Get them nice and wet," I demanded. With my coated thumb and finger, I gripped his right nipple, giving it a tug, then rolling it between my saliva-covered fingers. At the same time I was repeating the process with my other hand, getting his second nipple as aroused as the first. As my fingers dried, I became more forceful, beginning to squeeze and pluck them. Julian moaned, putting his hands behind himself, fumbling at my crotch, attempting to get my zipper open.

Pushing his hands away, I said, "Not yet," and instead undid his belt. Popping open the buttons on his jeans, I let his pants fall to the floor. He stood in front of me just in his briefs, my crotch pressed against his crack.

Taking his nipples back in my fingers, I gave them a squeeze, then leaned my mouth in beside his ear. "Are you ready for this?" I asked. He nodded. "Are you sure? Tell me you want it," I demanded.

"Please . . ." he panted.

I ran my fingernail around the ridge of his cock through his briefs, savoring the dampness that was already leaking out. I thrust a thumb in each side, lowering his briefs in a swift movement, exposing his cock to my exploring hand. I grasped it tightly, enjoying the feel of the sticky wetness that was oozing out of it. With my left hand, I gave one of his nipples a vicious tweak, and as he opened his mouth to let out a gasp I clamped my other hand over his lips. "Taste your juices," I whispered in his ear. "Lick them up. Soon it will be your come you will be tasting."

His tongue darted out, tentatively at first, then with more enthusiasm, as he consumed the pre-come he had been leaking, cleaning first the palm of my hand, then the fingers; one by one.

Deciding the time had come for my own enjoyment, I quickly removed my own clothing, all the while standing behind Julian, eyeing the curves of his ass. When I had completely stripped, I reached out and kneaded his cheeks, gradually pulling them apart to admire the delightful sight contained within them. I nestled my cock in his crack, resting it outside his hole, letting him feel what would later be inside him. I reached around and gave his dick a quick tug, and made sure it was still leaking, before guiding him to my bed.

Lying on my back, I pulled him towards me. He began to lie on top of me. "No," I stopped him, "Sit on my face." He straddled my head, his ass inches from my lips. His scrotum dangled on my chin, and I flicked my tongue out and up, giving it a quick taste, causing Julian to shudder in delight. Gently, I prized his cheeks apart, taking a look at his glorious hole from close up. Like his nipples, it was surrounded by a faint circle of hair. Only very lightly, though—certainly not the hairy mess that some men have, which would cause friction burns if one attempted to penetrate their hole. With Julian, it was just a light dusting—enough to be appealing but no more. I savored the sight for a long minute or two, then with my tongue licked a path up one of his cheeks, across the base of his spine and back down his other cheek to his scrotum. Again and again I repeated the process, making my circles ever so slightly smaller each time; homing in on his hole itself. The closer I got to the rim of his hole, the more he began to writhe above me, causing me to wrap one arm around his thighs. Taking a final deep breath, I pulled him down onto me, plunging my tongue into his hole.

It became apparent he was unused to being tongue-fucked—it was not long before he was bucking as though he were coming close to climaxing. I lifted his ass off my face, stopping my tongue action. "You ready for more?" I asked, reaching my arm out to a pack of condoms I keep beside my bed. He nodded enthusiastically. I tore a condom off and sheathed myself. "Turn around." I instructed. He turned, his legs straddling my stomach. I pressed a finger against his hole. It slid in easily, given the tongue-fucking it had just had. "You want me inside you?" I asked, slipping another finger inside him. He grunted, and nodded vigorously. I eased him back, letting my dick press against the outside of his sphincter. "You sure?" I teased.

He didn't wait any longer, and sat back, forcing the head of my dick inside him. I gave a groan as I felt the squelching pop of my dick breaking through. I slowly fed more of my shaft inside him, till I was buried to the hilt. Slowly, then with greater momentum, Julian began bouncing up and down, using the tight muscles of his ass to milk my cock. At the same time my hands were wandering over the front of his body, playing with his nipples, tracing the muscles of his stomach, massaging his thighs.

Eventually the grip of his hole began to work its magic, and I began to feel the pressure build in my balls. I took his cock in my hand, and began to stroke it in earnest. As he realized what I was doing, his bouncing slowed down, giving me some respite. "I want you to come," I demanded, increasing the tempo on his dick, while slowly easing myself in and out of his ass. My other hand was rapidly moving across his chest, tweaking one nipple, then the other. As the hand grasping his shaft moved faster and faster, I felt his body tense, and his hole began to contract around my dick. I began thrusting in time with his contractions.

"That's it," I instructed, "I want you to shoot all over me." Moments later, his body gave a shudder, and he was doing just that— spurting trails of come from my navel to my chin. Thick blobs covered my chest and stomach. As his breathing subsided, he closed his eyes, focusing on the feel of cock sliding in and out of his ass. As I felt myself getting close to the edge of coming myself, I used one hand to scoop up Julian's come, then the other to pull his jaw open. As he opened his eyes in surprise, I thrust my come-covered hand against his mouth. "Eat it . . ." I demanded. In shock, he tried to twist his head away, but I continued to hold my hand against his mouth; using my other hand to close off his nose, forcing his mouth open. His initial resistance, with all its bucking and twisting drove my dick wild, getting me closer and closer to the edge. Before long, though, he bowed to the inevitable and began to lick my hand clean. What began as apprehension soon turned into enthusiasm, and before long he was devouring every drop of his come. As he finished sucking down the last few bits, he reached down and began pulling on my nipples, eager to help finish me off. I felt my balls beginning to boil over, and gave a last deep thrust, working the length of my shaft into his hole. My back arching, I felt the dams burst; and a racing river of come soon filled the condom in Julian's ass.

With a sigh, I gently sank back onto the bed, pulling Julian down onto me. My softening dick popped out of his ass, as we gently kissed.

Pledge

M. Christian

The basement of the Gamma Alpha house: roughly cut floor beams for a ceiling, coarse concrete on the floor, paneling on the walls, light from a single bare bulb, members in their robes and hoods, the pledge in jeans and a simple T-shirt.

"Do you know why you're here?" Roger asked, voice pushed down as deep as it would go.

"Duh," the pledge said, a bright, wide smile on his boyish face. "I'm trying to get in."

Behind and around Roger, their faces under their hoods, their bodies under their robes, the other brothers grumbled and growled at the pledge's attitude.

"That's correct," Roger said, voice catching a bit. Choking down a cough, he continued, maybe a bit too fast: "You are pledging to join this noble house."

The pledge looked about to say something but then didn't.

"We are here, in this holy place"—another almost cough there—"to determine if you are worthy of joining our order."

The smile on the pledge's face didn't change: "Whatever."

Still behind and around Roger, their faces still gone under their hoods, their bodies still gone under their robes, the other brothers grumbled and growled even louder at the pledge's attitude.

"Do you feel you deserve to be part of this esteemed fraternity?" Roger demanded, trying to deepen his voice even lower, to get a weight of solemnity into the event.

"Better than a lot of things, I guess." The pledge said with a shrug and an even brighter, even wider, even more boyish grin.

Behind and around Roger, their faces continuing to be inscrutable under their hoods, their bodies continuing to be invisible under their robes, the other brothers grumbled and growled thunderously at the pledge's attitude.

"Before we can consider you for this house you must prove to us that you are worthy. Are you prepared to do that we ask of you, no matter how outrageous or humiliating?"

The pledge's smile didn't fade. If anything it grew in brightness and strength, the enamel of his smile making soft stars of the room's single bare bulb. "Yes," he said. "Yes, I am."

"Then remove your shoes and socks," Roger said. Somewhere behind him one of the robed brothers tittered, making the other robed brothers turn around looking for which of their order had broken the solemnity of the moment.

The pledge did as he was told. But he didn't just take off his shoes, then his socks. Or even, impossibly, his socks, then his shoes. Instead he ... well ... no other pledge in the history of Gamma Alpha house had ever taken his shoes and then his socks off in quite so remarkable a manner. It was like he danced them off, peeled them off, literally slipped them off.

Then the pledge was just standing, shoeless and sockless, on the bare concrete floor of the house.

Behind and around Roger, their faces remaining inscrutable under their hoods, their bodies remaining invisible under their robes, the other brothers were dead quiet at the pledge's attitude.

"Good," Roger said; this time his voice did catch, he did cough. Recovering as well as he could, he went on, trying even harder to lower his register into dire solemnity. "By doing this you've begun to expose your soul to the brotherhood. But we're not finished with you yet."

Almost too quick, almost too sharp, to be noticed, the pledge asked: "Soul?"

"Your shirt," Roger said, unsure what to say next as, for some reason, he'd strayed from the script. "Remove your shirt at once."

No hesitation, no shame, no nerves, no dread, no fear, no fright: the pledge's hands went to the bottom of his simple T-shirt and in one gesture he took it off. But he didn't just take off the shirt. Instead he . . . well . . . no other pledge in the history of Gamma Alpha house had ever taken his shirt off in quite so remarkable a manner. It was like he danced it off, peeled it off, literally slipped it off.

His shirt then joined his shoes and socks on the bare concrete floor of the house.

It wasn't merely the way he'd removed his shoes and then his socks, though that was part of it. It wasn't the way he'd taken off his shirt, though that played a role, too. It wasn't that he did it all casually, easily. It was that he'd done it like a dancer, or a chef, or someone who slipped things off with sly craft.

It was because he seemed to be enjoying himself.

Behind and around Roger, their faces staying inscrutable under their hoods, their bodies staying invisible under their robes, the other brothers thundered and bellowed at the pledge's attitude.

Roger turned around quickly, giving the pledge his robed back and his fellow brothers his front. Meeting a few of their eyes, he tried to intimidate them into backing up, shutting up, and giving the ceremony some seriousness.

"You are nothing," Roger said, working very hard to become very serious. "You are less than nothing."

The pledge's boyish face flashed comical confusion at what Roger had so seriously intoned. Behind Roger a few of his brothers, more than likely pissed at his recent chastising look, laughed too much and too loudly.

Roger's face bloomed red. "You're just a pledge. Just a fucking pledge. Now take off your fucking pants." He knew he'd said too much for the scene, said it too loudly, but he was too angry to care.

The pledge just smiled. Grinned, really: cat and canary kind of dental work. Dancing, again; cooking hot again; slipping clothing again, his fingers began to play nimbly with his button fly. It wasn't a long play, though, as his dance, his recipe, his sliding seemed to be set to a quicker tempo— either that or the boyish pledge was getting impatient as well.

But for a different reason.

The jeans descended, catching a bit on firm thighs before falling all the way down to the floor. Roger watched. The brothers did the same and the room got very quiet.

The pledge was more than handsome. His body seemed happy, pleasant, joyful, like it was an extension of his smile, his laugh, his glittering eyes.

For all of one minute, Roger didn't say anything.

Behind and around Roger, their faces static under their hoods, their bodies static under their robes, the other brothers were dead quiet, as well, at sight of the pledge in nothing but his shorts.

"Y-you stand before us as a pledge," Roger said, the loudness of his voice slamming in the still room. Embarrassed, he coughed into his hand before starting again: "You can either leave this room as member of the frat or as a reject, something even worse than a pledge: a total nothing—"

"But I thought a pledge already was nothing," the nearly naked young man pointed out, his already bright grin flashing a brilliant comedic white.

"Just shut the fuck up," came a Southern-flavored voice from over Roger's right shoulder. A slightly New York one came from the same direction but farther back: "Fucking asshole." One from the left side, but tinged with Minnesota, echoed with "Yeah, dickhead."

The pledge's grin faded a bit, slipped a tad. "Sorry," he said with a small voice, almost a whisper.

"Silence, Pledge," Roger said, trying to put it all back on track. He should have said it firmly, thunderously, but instead it came out soft, only echoing once rather than maybe twice in the tight confines of the frat basement.

The pledge's wider, kinder, sweeter smile returned and naturally, again playfully, he cocked his hips and hooked his thumbs into the elastic of his shorts.

Frozen behind and around Roger, their faces frozen under their hoods, their bodies frozen under their robes, the other brothers got quiet again at the pledge's stance.

"Do you want to join this order?" Roger asked, now completely off track, totally lost. But he felt he had to say something, so that's what he said.

The pledge, for some reason, actually took some time to answer. When he did his voice was remarkably cool, controlled, and aware: "It'd be nice to have some friends around here."

Behind and around Roger, their faces unmoving under their hoods, their bodies unmoving under their robes, the other brothers laughed like clever hyenas hearing a good joke.

The pledge's smile went from warm to cold, from friendly to reserved. His back arched, his jaw worked—back and forth, back and forth—then he took a good grip on the elastic of his shorts and yanked them down.

It happened fast, really fast. One moment they saw it, one moment they didn't.

Behind and around Roger, their faces shocked under their hoods, their bodies shocked under their robes, the other brothers were paralyzed by what they saw.

The pledge's cock went from one moment there, soft, to one moment not soft—hard. Hard, very, very hard.

Roger looked, watched, stared. He felt a deep tug, a muscular throb. Only tangentially he was aware that it was a very specific part of his body, a part that had responded about as quickly as the pledge's cock had.

Then he was aware that the pledge, too, was aware: the man who, technically, was nothing but a pledge was looking, watching, staring at the front of Roger's robe.

And he was smiling. Not coldly, not playfully, not mischievously, but with a joyous, close-to-beatific grin on his young face.

Then the brothers weren't static, frozen, unmoving, or shocked. As one, angry and outraged, frightened and disturbed, they rushed forward, fists emerging from under the anonymity of their robes.

Roger didn't think, he only did what he had to do: he stepped between them and the pledge.

A bench on campus: manicured lawn on the right, the left, and behind; gracefully undulating sidewalk in front; the pledge still in jeans and a T-shirt but not the T-shirt and jeans he'd worn two days before.

Roger came along the sidewalk, sitting without a pause next to the pledge.

Pledge

"So," the pledge said with a winsome smile, "I guess I didn't get in."

Roger returned the grin. "No, sorry."

"No big deal, I guess."

"If it makes you feel any better," Roger said, putting his hand out to be taken and shaken. "You didn't get in, but I came out."

The pledge, who wasn't a pledge anymore, of course, took Roger's hand. "Welcome, glad to have you as a member," he said.

It's All Greek to Me

Kale Naylor

The entire room spun when I raised my head from the pillow. Rubbing my eyes, I took a few deep breaths to combat the dizziness. It was when I reopened my eyes that I noticed that things weren't adding up. I wasn't in my room, and for the life of me I couldn't figure out whose room it was. It was too big to be a dorm room. And since when did I start sleeping in the buff? The first thing that came to mind was that I'd had a wild, drunken night, like most college freshmen. That would be true and quite cliché if it weren't for the fact that I was a lifelong straight-edger. It was then that I realized I wasn't the only person in the king-size bed. To my left was a sleeping, hulking blond breathing heavily with his back to me.

"Ah hell," I groaned.

I ran a hand through my shaggy brown hair and flopped back on the mattress as the vivid recollection of the previous night's events returned.

It was Friday afternoon and I was anxiously awaiting the weekend. Freshmen year had proven to be pretty manageable. Classes were a breeze and I had a laid-back job in the computer lab which allowed ample study time. Coming from a conservative background, I was pretty shy and low-key and had yet to attend a college party. Just wasn't my scene. I never went to a single party in high school and it looked like that trend was going to continue here in college. My biggest fear was that people would find out I was gay and would make my life a living hell. Such were the joys of living in the South. I emailed my English paper to my professor. I closed my laptop as I sighed. I was a free man for the next seventy-two hours. That moment, my roommate Chad burst through the door.

"Hey, Sean, you got to work tonight?" he asked.

"Uh, no," I replied. "What's up?"

"Sweet, we're going out tonight."

"No! I am not in the mood for having to get you out of jail."

"That was last month and the charges got dropped. Anyway, you're going out with me tonight."

"I appreciate the invitation but I already have plans."

"What, being a bookworm? Dude, you need to loosen up and live a little."

"And your problem is you have too much fun."

Chad nodded and scratched the dark stubble on his face.

"Yeah you're probably right," he said. "Just come out with me tonight. There's a toga party over at the Sigma house. I promise you'll have fun. Booze, babes, and I think they're hiring a DJ."

"Why the sudden interest in my social life?"

"I didn't realize you had one."

"Funny."

"I just want you to enjoy college. You're my bud and I don't want you having any regrets that you missed out on stuff."

I glared at Chad with a raised eyebrow. "You're so full of shit. Now I know you've got an ulterior motive."

Chad sighed and flopped down on his bed.

"Okay, you know I'm planning on pledging this semester."

"The Sigma Kappas, right?"

"Right. Well I was chatting with a couple of them over at the student center and your name came up."

"Really?"

"Yeah, apparently you helped one of the guys with their homework in the computer lab or something. One of them asked if I was your roommate and they invited us both to the toga party they're throwing tonight."

"I don't know . . ."

"Please, Sean. This could score me some serious points with the brothers. Do this and I promise I won't give you grief about partying again. Just make an appearance. If you're not having fun after an hour then you can take off. I'll make an excuse that you weren't feeling well or something. Please, bro."

"Well, I guess if you're trying to impress the frat brothers, I won't have to worry too much about you getting arrested again for indecent exposure."

"Yes, I promise to keep my pants on too. Unless I manage to score some alone time with Katie Milligan. Hehehehehe."

For the life of me I couldn't think of any specific episode where I helped out one of the Sigmas. The computer lab didn't get many Greeks or, for that matter, jocks. They usually only appeared in the labs around midterms and finals. The only person I could think of was that mysterious blond who regularly came into the lab. With hypnotic dark green eyes and that bright gorgeous smile, which he often showcased, I was always too eager to help him out the few times he had problems with his PC. Though he possessed the preppy frat boy Abercrombie look, he didn't have the stereotypical attitude. He was modest, articulate, and very personable. A far cry from the pack of arrogant, obnoxious Cro-Mags whose ranks my roommate wanted to join. In all likelihood the guy (if this was the guy) was probably straight and had a girlfriend, some cheerleader or sorority babe or something. Just the same, this party might be worthwhile after all.

That evening, I gave myself a once-over in the bathroom mirror. I zipped up my hoodie and adjusted my glasses. While a bit on the thin side, I considered myself fairly cute. I definitely had the baby face and looked younger than eighteen.

"You ready, Seanster?" Chad asked.

"Yeah."

I headed for the door when Chad grabbed my shoulder.

"Hang on, bud," he said. "We can't have you making me look bad."

He removed my glasses, adjusted my hoodie, and ruffled my hair.

"Much better," he said. "Let's roll."

The blaring rap music and the mob of students on the Sigma Theta Kappa house lawn indicated that the toga party was well underway. We weaved through the hundreds of people gathered as we made our way into the house.

"Thanks for coming again," Chad yelled over the noise.

"Don't mention it," I said.

"Listen, if you need anything give me a holler."

Before I could respond, my roommate had vanished into the crowd. Several scantily clad coeds stood atop tables and gyrated to the music. Judging by the bills poking out of their waistbands, they clearly were putting themselves through college as exotic dancers. To my right, a group of guys cheered their buddy on as he licked salt from a girl's taut belly and took a shot of tequila. In one corner, a group of guys cheered as two chicks made out and groped each other. I tried not to stare too long as a group of buff toga-clad Sigmas drew near. With well-sculpted chests and biceps, the thin bedspreads from their makeshift costumes provided a nice outline of their nicely shaped cocks and asses. My jeans suddenly became very snug. I needed to cool off. These Greeks were nothing like their namesakes of yore, and the last thing I needed was to piss off a pack of homophobic frat boys. I turned around and that's when I spotted him. I barely recognized him due to the blue backwards baseball cap on his head. Across the room, near the staircase, the enigmatic blond locked lips with and fondled the breasts of some petite redhead. True to form, he had a girlfriend.

"So much for that fantasy," I said.

I headed for the bar.

"What's your poison?" asked the bartender.

"Just a soda."

The bartender gave me a suspicious look.

"Designated driver," I lied.

He nodded and handed me a Coke in a plastic cup. I wasn't in the mood for catching any shit about being a pansy nondrinker. I took a sip before staring at the lesbian action that continued in the corner.

"Having fun?" asked a familiar voice.

My eyes widened when I realized it was the blond—minus the girlfriend.

"Yeah," I lied. "Having a blast."

"Cool," he said. "We try to make sure everyone has fun at our parties, specifically those who help us out in the computer lab."

"So you're a Sig?"

"Yeah. I thought you knew."

I shook my head, "I don't think I've ever introduced myself. I'm Sean."

"I'm Cody."

"Are all your parties this crazy?"

"You should check out the action over at the Jacuzzi. Some of the Chi babes are making out with each other and some of my brothers. You should definitely stop by and hop in."

"I don't have a bathing suit."

He flashed his trademark smile. "Neither do they."

It was then that my body began buzzing. I was feeling warm and lightheaded. More to the point, I was feeling good and very horny. What the hell was happening?

"You all right there?" he asked.

"Yeah," I said, breathing heavily. "I think I just need to sit down for a minute."

I stumbled as I attempted to walk away. Cody caught me and wrapped my arm around his neck.

"Come on, bud," he said. "Let's get you out of here."

Cody escorted me through the crowded room and up the stairs.

"He's fine—had too much to drink," he repeated to onlookers.

We eventually arrived at his room and Cody deposited me on top of his bed.

"I should probably head home," I slurred.

Cody smiled as he pressed me back to the bed. He walked to his door and locked it. He then moved to his dresser, turned on the radio, and cranked up the volume.

"Don't know what's wrong," I said. "I didn't drink."

"Don't worry," he said. "It's probably too much excitement. You just need to cool off and rest. Let's get you out of these clothes."

My heart began pounding in my chest. My entire body buzzing, I was rock hard and I didn't want him to discover it.

"That's okay," I replied weakly. "Really . . . not . . . necessary."

Cody ignored my protests and continued to strip me. I was too out of it to mount any resistance. I was clad in only my boxer briefs when Cody stopped to admire his handiwork.

"Very nice," he said. "You clearly work out regularly."

I didn't, but why correct him?

"And what is this?" Cody asked. He removed my final article of clothing. "Very nice."

Cody continued to massage my cock. The jolt of pleasure from the ministrations was making me even more turned on than I already was. It was a miracle I didn't come right then and there.

"I was hoping your roommate would talk you into showing up tonight," he said.

"What? Why?" I asked, fighting to remain coherent.

"I thought it was obvious with all of those trips to the computer lab and me constantly asking for help." He whispered in my ear, "I really want to fuck you."

"Your girlfriend?"

"What? You mean Tracy? Please. She's just a piece of ass I tap every once in awhile."

"You're gay?"

"Bi. And as much as I enjoy pussy, girls are just too fragile. There are just some things you can do with guys that you could never do with girls. Such as getting a nice piece of ass nice and relaxed so I can fuck him senseless."

"What?"

"Yeah, I had the bartender, Darren, slip you a cocktail. A little something to get you to relax. I've seen all the times you've checked me out. You've wanted this for a long time but were too scared to go after it."

"Your frat?"

"Oh, you mean my brothers? Yeah they know about me. They're cool with it. They know I'm a sex-hound who swings both ways. Hell I've even fucked a few of them. On top of that I'm a legacy. So, yeah, no worries."

He began to remove his shirt, slowly, watching my eyes gleam as his broad and well-muscled chest was exposed. My breathing became more labored as he removed the remainder of his clothing. He finally removed his boxers, revealing his long, hard manhood. He was completely nude save for his backwards baseball cap, his necklace and a brown leather bracelet. His pale chiseled body was practically hairless.

"We can't," I weakly protested. "We shouldn't."

With a beaming grin, he straddled my waist. "Your cock says otherwise."

He grabbed my chin and kissed me. My inhibitions lowered from the drug, and overcome with lust, I conceded and allowed him to dominate me. He planted kisses on my neck and descended down my torso and licked at my abs. I gasped as I felt his caresses descend even further. Moans slipped from my mouth as Cody slurped and sucked away at my cock.

"Oh God," I groaned.

"Knew you'd like that."

Cody mercilessly licked away at my neck and ear. In response I ran my hand through his blond mane. Cody expertly slid his tongue around each of my nipples before giving each one a light bite. He grinned as he heard me moan.

"And I'm just getting started," he said.

He flipped me over on my stomach and lightly ran his tongue from my earlobe to the small of my back. Massaging my ass, Cody parted my cheeks and teased the ring of my hole with his tongue. I gritted my teeth and clinched the sheets with all of my strength as Cody worked me over. Without warning, the Sigma brother plunged his long thick cock into my ass.

"Oh, God!" I gasped.

"Damn, you're tight as hell," Cody moaned. "I'm going to enjoy fucking you on a regular basis."

It's All Greek to Me

Sweat poured off our bodies and drenched the sheets. I panted heavily as Cody pumped his cock into my ass. It didn't take him long to hit my prostate and after that I groaned for more. With his hands firmly planted on my hips, Cody repeatedly thrust into me while I in turn lunged back to match each assault. My mind was ravaged with lust and the only thing I wanted—more than breathing—was this blond stud to fuck me senseless. Eventually we found a rhythm and fucked to the beat of the rock song playing from Cody's stereo.

"I'm getting close," he moaned.

Little did he realize that I was close, too. My balls began to tighten up as his dick continuously assaulted my prostate. The fucking was so intense that I had yet to even touch my cock. As if reading my mind, Cody reached around and gripped my swollen organ. A couple strokes were all it took. I cried as my cock discharged a steady stream of come. A few additional thrusts and Cody shot inside of me. Sweating and gasping for breath, the two of us collapsed on top of the bed. His arm draped across my chest, Cody lay next to me and the two of us drifted off to sleep.

As I lay there the next morning, guilt immediately kicked in. I'd let some frat boy use me for a one-night stand. He had me and nabbed another notch under his belt. Worst of all was that I'd enjoyed it. I surmised that he was done with me and would kick me out of his room and humiliate the hell out of me. To save myself the indignity of being discarded like week-old-trash, I decided it was best for me to make my exit before he woke up. Hopefully I would manage to sneak out of the Sigma House unnoticed and not arouse any suspicion. I bent over and reached for my boxer briefs when a pair of arms coiled around my waist and yanked me back on top of the bed. Still groggy from the cocktail Cody had slipped me, I was too weak to struggle as a giggling Cody straddled me once again.

"You weren't planning on leaving, were you?" he asked with his signature smile. "Because that would be rude."

"I think I need to leave."

"Why would you want to do that? I had a blast last night, and quite frankly I was looking for an encore. Several in fact."

I attempted to push him off but he simply pinned my wrists to the bed. He giggled as I struggled futilely.

"Get off!" I ordered.

"That's what I'm trying to do."

"You drugged me, you asshole."

"I loosened you up. It wasn't like you were unconscious. I just helped you lower your walls. I wouldn't have done it if I thought you weren't game. You're so damn uptight, nothing short of a party favor would've loosened you up."

"I'm going to kill Chad."

"Your roommate wasn't in on it. I figured you were still in the closet and I didn't want to out you. As far as he knows, I was only inviting two freshmen to a frat party. Don't worry. I know he's been wanting to pledge our fraternity. I'll see to it that he gets in."

Ignoring him, I continued to struggle, to no avail.

"Okay, so maybe I went a little extreme."

"You think?"

"But I wouldn't have gone through all of this trouble if I didn't think you were worth it. I think you're a really nice guy and not just another lay. And I'm not that bad a guy. And tell me you didn't have fun. Or tell me that you don't want to fuck me again."

"That certainly won't be happening."

He leaned in and whispered in my ear, "That wasn't an answer, but answer me this. If you really didn't enjoy yourself or don't want another go, how come you're rock hard right now?"

I rolled my eyes in defeat. He had me there. Before I could offer a retort, he began licking my ear and grinding against my cock.

"Stop . . . wait," I said between breaths. "All right, it was fun, but you can't just take advantage and . . . Oh, fuck it!"

I pushed Cody onto his back and immediately devoured his cock. He placed his hands behind his head and smiled as I gave him one of the most frenzied blowjobs ever. It was late Saturday evening when we finally staggered out of the room.

Cody—and for that matter, Chad—was right about one thing. I was too uptight and needed to live a little. Cody kept true to his word and Chad became a Sigma. Suffice to say I attended a lot more parties at the frat house and was a regular visitor. The cover story was that I was stopping by to hang out with Chad and Cody, but based on the wry looks I regularly got from Darren and several of the brothers, I'm pretty sure they knew better.

Roomies

Michael Roberts

I left college when I was twenty and went back when I was thirty-eight.

You may wonder why I let so much time elapse between periods of academic pursuit, but even if you don't, this is my story, so I'm going to tell you anyway.

I stopped after two years of higher education because my college raised its tuition, and simultaneously, my family and I suffered a few financial setbacks. I couldn't afford to stay in school.

I returned to my small hometown in Colorado to work in the family business—auto repair—and watched with a certain feeling of helplessness as my life kept taking unanticipated twists and turns: marriage; the realization that perhaps I wasn't cut out for the wedded state; a divorce that was weepy and waily for both my wife and me, followed by several years of alimony until she remarried, followed as well by several years of searching my progressively perplexed soul, and awkward, clandestine experiments in lust with other men—the clichés of sexual confusion.

Of course, it wasn't cliché to me as I struggled through the quicksand of my existence.

I guess that in a way, I was trying to recapture a less-complicated period when I decided to attend college again and, at the same time, to remove myself from the claustrophobia of a place where I couldn't take a step without running into someone I knew—family, friends, my ex-wife's friends, repair shop customers. And, more problematically, co-couplers. Even though the men with whom I briefly conspired in underground erotic encounters were not numerous, they happened to often be nearby. Some man and I popped up together, as it were, and then he constantly popped up at my garage, at restaurants, at grocery stores, on street corners. And even if we both managed to be circumspect, it was, I thought, only a matter of time before we gave something away by our obvious attempts to not give anything away.

While thirty-eight was more than a bit late to be changing direction, I knew that I couldn't continue tinkering with car motors. I wanted to finish my degree in political science and then do something else—I wasn't sure what, but something.

Although limited by the burden of alimony and by helping my family back to stability, I finally managed to save enough money to continue college, especially if I could find ways to curtail expenses and get into a work-study program. It was time—past time—to take a few chances.

My second departure for academe wasn't like the first—no enthusiastic good wishes, no expressions of pride as the adventurer marched off to scale the mountains of knowledge. Just puzzled head-shaking as I set out on my quixotic endeavor.

I confess that my head was shaking a bit, too, as well as my knees. Anticipation and anxiety alternately dominated, and more than once, I was intensely tempted to wheel my car around and retreat to relative security.

But I drove on. As I somewhat melodramatically put it to myself, I needed to find out who I really was—sexually, intellectually, personally.

I arrived on campus feeling as if I'd crossed a border into a foreign country in which I didn't know the language or the geography or the customs. I asked someone how to get to Maxwell Hall and received a strange look—why, I could hear him asking himself, was this old fart wondering how to get to a dorm? Staying at a campus residence was one of the ways I was cutting economic corners. I'd arranged for a private room, which was still less expensive than an apartment.

Maxwell's lobby was full of both guys and gals waiting for room assignments. This evidently was a coed dorm, which I hadn't anticipated—one more adjustment I was going to have to make to a collegiate environment different from the one I'd lived in nearly twenty years ago. The front desk clerk was too harried to take any notice of me as different from the rest of the teeming multitude. I realized, with something of a jolt, that I was old enough to be the father of a lot of these kids; no doubt many people assumed that indeed I was just another parent settling his child.

I took the elevator upstairs and found the room number I'd been assigned. I opened the door and discovered a young man putting sheets on one of the two beds.

"Oh," I said, flummoxed—or, rather, more flummoxed than I'd already been—"there must be some mistake." Or, rather, yet another mistake in a series that had begun when I'd chosen to enroll again in school.

The young man had on jeans and a T-shirt that accentuated a well-defined body, especially as he bent over the bed and stretched to tuck in a sheet corner. His blond hair was closely cropped, and his eyes were an aquatic shade of blue. His look was open and friendly, like a model on the cover of a college catalog assuring prospective students of the perfect academic experience.

"Are you Tim?" he asked.

I thought about it.

"Yes," I answered.

"I'm Gregory, your roommate."

"There's been a mistake," I said again, just in case I hadn't made myself clear. "I'm supposed to be single. Well, I am single—now, anyway—but I mean, I'm supposed to have a single room."

I knew that I was on the verge of babbling. And I knew, too well, why. The basic situation, of course, was strange, and finding myself with someone who claimed to be my roommate added to my discomfort. It didn't help my discombobulation that this potential roommate was half my age and damned good looking.

"—and he said"—I realized Gregory was continuing—"that there'd been some confusion—"

"Who said?" I interrupted.

"Harold, the desk clerk—he said that I was going to be with some dude who wanted to be alone—too many applicants for too few rooms, I guess—and you and I'd be together, and I should tell you, because he wouldn't remember. Okay?"

"Well," I answered, and stopped. After a moment of silence in which Gregory and I stared at each other, he said, "Good."

He tossed a pillow onto the bed. "I hope you don't mind that I made myself at home before you got here. I'm going out to meet some friends, so I'll see you later."

At the door, he paused and grinned at me with, it seemed, about twice as many teeth as anybody should have, blindingly.

"It'll be all right, Tim," he said. "I'm a very nice guy. You'll like me."

Then my whirlwind roommate was gone.

And I reflected that I already did like him—and that was a problem.

That first quarter, I congratulated myself that I exercised more self-discipline than I'd thought I possessed. Some of these congratulations were to encourage myself to keep up the discipline.

It wasn't easy.

He *was* a nice guy. He was outgoing and friendly, and at the same time, he respected our age difference, his nineteen to my thirty-eight. If he resented sharing a room with me instead of a guy closer to his own age, he didn't show it.

I often felt an eon or two beyond my years, sitting in classes with students who were in their early twenties, hoping that my contributions to discussions were intelligent and didn't sound like some fuddy-duddy opinions that should be consigned to the scrapheap of the hopelessly out-of-date. At least occasionally I thought that the younger professors and some fellow scholars alike were patronizing someone they felt should have left the acquiring of knowledge to those whose brains hadn't turned to cornmeal mush.

Gregory—I discovered early that he preferred the full version of his name—sometimes helped me with my studies, and sometimes I was able to help him. I would stand beside him in his chair at his desk, leaning over to point out an item in a textbook, and I inhaled his youth, and I often felt like a dirty old man in a particularly bad joke, because he *was* a nice guy, and he was bright and gregarious and deferential—and did I mention young and beautiful? I wanted him so much that I feared that any discretion I was managing to maintain was going to dissolve when I finally started drooling.

In my hometown, my partners had been whatever my age was at a given time. Yet here, suddenly, inexplicably, in my middle age, I was becoming entranced by a younger guy I'd just met.

Well, perhaps somewhat explicably. Close quarters had something to do with my fixation—a nicer term than obsession. Whether he was wearing jeans that tantalizingly hid his still obviously well-formed legs or gym shorts that revealed muscular thighs; whether his torso was encased in a T-shirt that strained as he leaned back and forth over his work or was uncovered and gleaming with nipples perpetually perky; whether he was sitting, standing, or lying down, I found it difficult not to stare at him.

When he stood beside me in nothing but white briefs, I couldn't resist glances at his rounded crotch.

I awoke early one morning and noticed him in bed with his covers tossed off, clad in boxers with the fly gaping. I in turn gaped like an explorer trying to see what was hidden inside a cave. I thought that I caught the moment his eyes opened, and I snapped mine shut, and a few minutes later, I opened my eyes and ostentatiously stretched and yawned and wondered if my charade had worked. At least he didn't rise theatrically and accuse me of being a repulsive letch. It seemed that my secret was still safe.

Then it was the day of what might be called The Nude Sighting.

I hurried to the room one afternoon because in the lobby, I was suddenly seized with an almost irresistible need to piss. I pushed open the door to our room, glad that it was unlocked, and heard the shower running and saw that the bathroom door was ajar.

"Uh—Gregory," I called, "I really have to use the facilities." I cursed my attack of coyness.

"Go ahead," his voice answered. "I'm almost done."

"Uh—okay."

I hurried into the bathroom, unzipped so quickly that I nearly injured myself, pulled out my prick and turned it on.

I was glad that the shower curtain was opaque, so I couldn't stare through it and lose track of what I was doing and douse myself with urine. But as relief started, he turned off the shower, and I watched his hand appear from behind the plastic daffodils and daisies to grab a towel. I tried to pee faster. There was a ratcheting noise as the hooks slid across the metal bar, and I could no longer keep from looking at the shower stall. There he stood, wiping his face with one end of the towel, and the rest of it dropped down in front of him, covering the middle part of his body. At each side of the towel was a strip of flesh revealing the pelvic creases leading to his masked groin. I pissed more emphatically, hoping that I could manage a dick that was becoming hard.

Then he flipped the towel behind him and rubbed his back, revealing himself in all his splendor, and he was quite splendid. His cock was very pleasantly constructed, and one of his full balls grazed the tip, and as he dried himself, his prick swung left and right hypnotically. He grinned at me, dazzlingly, and exited the bathroom. He did not seem to notice, I was glad to see, that I was drizzling all over my shoes—maybe urine, but I wasn't sure.

By the time I finished washing my trembling hands and finally summoned the courage to leave the bathroom, Gregory had dressed and gone.

I sat down weakly on my bed and cursed the idea that I'd wanted to continue my education. I had managed to combine at least two parts of the formula of porno stories: the libido-driven older man lusting after the young hunk and the college student pining for his clueless roomie.

And as the next scene of my erotic extravaganza, I unzipped again and hauled out a cock that was already adhering to my underwear and jerked off, quickly, before Gregory returned.

Everything considered, I was glad when the quarter concluded.

I hadn't yet settled into the rigors of preparing for tests and writing papers. I wondered if I would adjust before year's end, if I ever would adjust, or if I was doomed to struggle until I managed to eke out my degree—if I did.

Gregory's distracting presence didn't help my study habits, such as they were. Even his absence disrupted the little concentration I was able to muster, because I anticipated seeing him again. I was too old, I told myself, to fixate on someone who was a comparative youngster, who couldn't possibly, I told myself, in any way return my attention.

I didn't know what his "romantic" interests were. He didn't spend all of his time in the dorm room, of course. I didn't ask where'd he been and with whom, and he didn't volunteer the information.

Gregory and I had an occasional drink or cup of coffee together, but I realized that I was not really part of his social life. That was to be expected, I told myself, since he was an attractive young man and I was middle-aged and feeling progressively more fossilized.

But no matter how many times I told myself all of these things, and no matter how carefully I listened, my heart still beat the faster in his presence, and my desire pulsed the more intensely, as if, at this belated stage of my life, I were experiencing my first crush.

So I was happy—in some regards, at least—to get away from campus and college life and even Gregory and go back home for the first quarter break that extended into Thanksgiving.

The vacation was one of mixed blessings. I enjoyed being with my family; I even felt somewhat nostalgic seeing my ex-wife. I contacted some of my former fuck buddies, and we did what fuck buddies do. Sometimes I was able to squelch the fantasies that I was with Gregory, and only once at the height of passion did I call out Gregory's name.

And then, finally and too soon, second quarter was going to start. With a confusing amalgam of emotions, I returned to school.

When I arrived, Gregory was already in our room.

"Hi, guy," I said, perhaps a bit too enthusiastically, too fast, at too high a pitch.

"Hello, Tim," he responded with a decided lack of energy.

"How was vacation?" I enquired, setting my suitcases on my bed.

"This isn't working," he said.

"Pardon me?"

"This isn't working," he repeated. "I'm going to ask for a transfer to another room."

"But how . . . ?" I asked. "But what . . . but why . . . ?" I concluded.

Gregory shook his head.

"I've tried every way I could think of to let you know I'm interested."

"Interested in what?"

"Interested in you."

"But how . . . but what . . . but . . . ?" I countered.

"All of the times I stood beside you in just my shorts when we studied together, and I'd dangle myself in front of you, but you never seemed to notice. That day in the bathroom when I was nude right there, you didn't even blink."

"Oh, I blinked." I was going to tell him about my epic pissing when we were in the bathroom together, but I decided that might not be a good idea.

He looked unconvinced.

"When I arrived here," I said, "I was . . . disconcerted . . . to find you in what I thought was going to be my room alone. I was . . . disconcerted . . . because you were there and because you were handsome . . . and still are, of course. And I was twice your age . . . I still am, of course. And I couldn't, wouldn't presume that you would return . . . you know? And it seemed best to do nothing. You know?"

"Not really."

"Oh, dude!" I said. I really said that. I couldn't believe I said that. But I did say that.

He looked at me as if I'd suddenly started speaking gibberish.

Right then, all of my restraint flew away like a badly trained bird.

"I didn't react because I was afraid to react," I rushed on. "The first time I saw you, I wanted you. And I didn't want you to know that I wanted you, because I didn't want to want you." Restraint was about to be replaced by incoherence. "I mean—Gregory, I'm twice your age," I said again, and added, in case I hadn't been clear, "You're half as old as I am."

"I like older men," he said, and his voice was soft, and his eyes had turned softer, and I was turning hard.

"But I didn't realize that. I didn't even know if you were gay, and evidently you are, and I don't know how you figured out I was gay—am gay—but it doesn't matter. All of those times you were so close to me . . . and sometimes barely dressed . . . . and sometimes not dressed at all . . . and your body was—is—so—" I flapped my hands in an attempt to convey his body's qualities. "And you're attractive—and I—and you're a nice guy, you've said so yourself—and I—oh, Gregory, I really—"

He held up a hand as if directing the traffic of my words.

"I think we should stop talking," he said.

Then he began unbuttoning his shirt, and I felt as if I were on a great height, dazed and lightheaded, and I watched transfixed as he took off his shirt and rolled his T-shirt up over his head and tossed them on his bed, and once again, I was stunned by the muscular glories of his chest, and then he slipped off his shoes and socks and unzipped his pants and stepped out of them, again unveiling his impressive legs, and then, oh, and then, he slid down his shorts onto the floor, and if his cock had been delightful when it was hanging so tastily as he left the shower, it was really quite wonderful when it was stretching straight out from his groin toward me, and he said, "Don't you suppose . . . ?" and I did suppose, and I practically ripped off my clothes, seeing and hearing unmoored buttons popping across the room, tossing to the side shoes that I'd wrenched off still tied, tangling myself in my T-shirt as I tugged it over my head, nearly falling as I removed my socks, doing a strange little dance as I got out of my trousers, and I was grateful that I'd kept myself in reasonably good shape, and when I pulled off my shorts, my dick, so rigid that it felt like iron, sprang from my crotch and gestured in a very friendly manner to his cock.

"Well," I said, and grinned.

"Well," he said, and grinned back, and then he was in my arms, and his mouth was twined with mine, and our cocks were crossed against each other, and his wetness anointed my stomach.

As if we were in a film with several frames missing, he was suddenly on his knees before me, and he took my cock in his mouth, and I gasped and rose up on my feet, *en pointe* in our ballet of lust.

He may have been young, but his technique lacked nothing. It was full of fire and finesse.

He was speedy, and he was slow; he devoured every inch of me, and he flicked the tip of my dick with his tongue; he went up and down my excited extension; he nibbled at my nuts and ingested them completely; he sprinted along the sensitive fleshway below my balls, and his rabbit of a tongue scurried into the warren of my asshole, and he delighted me almost unendurably.

Then Gregory smiled up at me, and we lay down top to bottom, and we ate of each other; I anchored my mouth on his cock so that I wouldn't float away in sheer pleasure. He tasted rich and robust; his cock had the flavor of youth; it was satiny solid and light and heavy; his tongue led me to the brink of release and rested and when I had subsided began anew; I skated over his length and breadth and took in his abundant sacs and delved into the fragrant flavorful fissure of his ass; I encircled the peak of his prick, and a rivulet of sweet juice flowed onto my tongue.

Gregory let go of me and rolled onto his back. He lifted his legs, and his cheeks parted like curtains, revealing the leading player in this drama of dormitory decadence.

I moved behind him. I held his ankles in my hands and looked down at his face. His eyes were glowing, and his grin seemed to cover his face.

I positioned the head of my dick at his gateway and pressed forward. His asshole sheathed my cock, and he tilted his head and closed his eyes and hummed a hum of pain and pleasure.

I entered him slowly, easing into his warmth. He opened his eyes and smiled up at me, and I wanted to take him quickly and utterly, and I had to exercise every bit of the minimal self-control I still had to keep my moderate tempo. When I was completely inside him, he closed his eyes again and whispered, "Yes, oh, yes," and he clasped me tightly.

His exuberant cock stretched up toward his navel, dividing the spheres of his succulent balls.

I extracted nearly all of my cock and then glided back into him, and again, and again, determinedly sustaining a moderate rhythm, but I could feel my constraint ebbing, and I attacked faster and faster, propelling my prick in and out of his ass, and he held onto my arms and met each thrust and curled his legs around my backside and urged me into him.

We were absolutely in tune; he wanted what I was giving, and I wanted the gifts that he was offering.

My fervor increased, and I threw myself into him and he surrendered to me, and it wasn't only two bodies combining, it was that I wanted, cared for, Gregory, and Gregory was sharing himself with me. He was saying, "Yes, Tim, yes, Tim, yes, yes, yes," and his dick was bouncing against his crotch, and my speed and force intensified, and his breathing became louder and more rapid, and he lifted his head and cried out, "Tim—yes—oh," and the come spurted out of his cock, fountained up over his stomach and chest, and he clutched me deep within him, and I was entirely sensation, wrenching and wracking, and I sighed, "Gregory," and shot into him, wave after exhilarating, exhausting wave.

I crumpled onto him, and we lay together, spent, for minutes, hours, until I stickily lifted myself and rolled over to lie beside him.

"So?" he said.

"So," I replied weakly.

"I think," he said, "that we're going to have a very good second quarter."

"I think," I said, "that I agree."

We did.

About the Contributors

A native Californian, **Bearmuffin** lives in San Diego with two leatherbears in a stimulating ménage à trois. He once dormed with the captain of the wrestling team at USC. These days he writes erotica for *Honcho* and *Torso*. His work is featured in several anthologies from Alyson Books.

Anne Cain is a graphic artist and writer with a passion for gay romance. She's written a number of short stories and novellas celebrating love between men, and recently contributed to Alyson's *Island Boys* anthology. Whenever she's not chained to the PC or doodling away in a sketchbook, she's curled up on the couch with her cats and a good read. To learn more about her stories and artwork, please visit her DeviantArt portfolio at http://annecain .deviantart.com/.

Zachary Chase spent his high school years being called a fag by the football team. However, once he began college, those very same football players all joined fraternities and would fool around with him after one too many keg parties.

M. Christian's numerous stories have appeared in such anthologies as *Best American Erotica*, *Best Gay Erotica*, *Best Lesbian Erotica*, as well as in the collections *Dirty Words*, *Speaking Parts*, *The Bachelor Machine*, and *Filthy*. He is also the author of the novels *Running Dry*, *The Very Bloody Marys*, *The Painted Doll*, and *Brushes*. But he is not—repeat NOT—the author of the novel *Me2*, despite what you might have heard.

About the Contributors

Paul A. Cooper is thirty-six years old and lives on the Gulf Coast with his partner of eleven years. His short story "Getting to Know My Neighbor" appears in the anthology *Ultimate Gay Erotica 2008*, published by Alyson Books.

Joe Filippone is a student at Red Rocks Community College majoring in psychology and criminal justice. He is the author of the plays *Mama's Boy, Lucille, After Saturday* and *The League of the Super-de-Duper-Uber-Good Guys* (2006 RMTA Playwrighting Competition Finalist). He is also the author of the short screenplay *Buddy's Confession* and the coauthor of the screenplay *Diner Stories*. His short stories have appeared in *Best Gay Love Stories: Summer Flings* (Alyson Books) as well as other forthcoming anthologies. www.myspace.com/hiphopjoe.

Marcus James is the author of *Blackmoore* and the fourth coming sequel *Symphony for the Devil*. He has contributed to numerous Alyson anthologies, including *Ultimate Gay Erotica 2007, Best Gay Love Stories: New York City,* and *Summer Flings,* as well as *Tales of Travelrotica for Gay Men Volume 2*. He is twenty-three years old. He can be reached at www.myspace.com/marcus_james and www.marcusjamesbooks.com. He lives in Phoenix.

Thom Jaymes attended college in West Virginia. He was not in a fraternity, but that didn't stop him from wondering what really went on behind those closed doors.

Anthony Lectito is an Australian author and bookseller. He holds an MA (Writing & Literature). While a typical day of bookselling is not quite like his story, he does have a thing for bibliophiles. He would love dearly to meet Witi Ihimaera in the flesh.

About the Contributors

Kale Naylor is an Atlanta, Ga. native who has been a freelance author/artist for a number of years. An All-American frat boy himself, many of Naylor's stories are based on his real-life misadventures.

Stephen Osborne attended Purdue University and was once nearly arrested for swimming naked in the main court's fountain. Hey, it seemed like the right thing to do at the time. He's had stories published in *Ultimate Gay Erotica 2008, Unmasked, Hard Hats, Best Gay Love Stories: Summer Flings, My First Time Volume 5, Dorm Porn 2,* and many others. He resides in Indianapolis with his fantastic roommate Frank and Jadzia the Wonder Dog. He is currently at work on a book of true ghost stories.

Neil Plakcy is the author of *Mahu, Mahu Surfer,* and *Mahu Fire,* mystery novels which take place in Hawaii. He is coeditor of *Paws & Reflect: A Special Bond Between Man and Dog* (Alyson Books, 2006) and editor of the gay construction worker erotica anthology *Hard Hats.* He did not pledge a fraternity in college, but now wishes he had.

Michael Roberts steps into the *Frat Sex* series after contributing to the *Dorm Porn* series. His work has also appeared in the Alyson anthology *Ultimate Gay Sex 2007.* Under various pseudonyms, he has also been published in several national gay magazines.

Rob Rosen, a proud alumnus of Phi Gamma Delta, is the author of the critically acclaimed novel *Sparkle: The Queerest Book You'll Ever Love.* His short stories have appeared in more than fifty anthologies to date, and his erotic fiction can frequently be found in the pages of *MEN, Freshmen,* and *[2]* magazines. Please visit him at his website, www.therobrosen.com, or email him at robrosen @therobrosen.com.

Simon Sheppard went to an avant-garde college without a single fraternity. Since then, he has written *In Deep: Erotic Stories*; *Kinkorama: Dispatches From the Front Lines of Perversion*; *Sex Parties 101*; and the award-winning *Hotter Than Hell and Other Stories*. He has edited *Homosex: Sixty Years of Gay Erotica* and *Leathermen*. His work also appears in well over 250 anthologies, including many editions of *The Best American Erotica* and *Best Gay Erotica*. He writes the syndicated column "Sex Talk" and the online serial "The Dirty Boys Club," and hangs out at www .simonsheppard.com.

Troy Storm, who considers himself a frat sex gourmet, has had several hundred gay, straight, and bi erotic short stories published in various magazines and anthologies, including Alyson's *Men for All Seasons, Full Body Contact, Frat Sex*, and the freshly buffed *Island Boys*.

Zavo was born and raised in the wooded hills of New England. Here he attended a two-year and a four-year college, the latter where his roommate pledged and became a member of a fraternity. This gave him plenty of exposure to hazing events as well as fraternity life overall. He is now ensconced in the rugged hills of the Northwest, where the solitude continues to feed his imagination to pen tales of lust, adventure, and unrequited love.